SUGAR ENFORCER

SUGAR DADDIES #14

CHARITY PARKERSON

Punk
&
Sissy

--Warning: This book is intended for readers over the age of 18.

Copyright © 2019 Charity Parkerson
Editor: Hercules Editing & Consultants
ISBN: 978-1-946099-54-9

INTRODUCTION

WHISKEY LIVES FOR JUSTICE. JUSTICE DOLES
IT OUT.

In an attempt to live more openly, Whiskey takes a chance on a local club. He's worked the neighborhood for fifteen years as a police detective, but never interacted much with the community. It doesn't take long to discover he doesn't fit in. Luckily, Justice swoops in and everything about Whiskey's life changes.

Meeting Whiskey wasn't an accident. It was a calculated move on Justice's part. Whiskey has been asking questions Justice needs him to stop asking. Months of watching Whiskey lets him know Whiskey can't be bought. Not with money anyhow. Justice has other ways to keep Whiskey occupied, and he's not opposed to using every trick in his arsenal to get his way.

Two men from opposites sides of the law. Feelings that can't be denied. It's a recipe guaranteed to blow up in everyone's face, and they might not survive the fallout.

ONE

THIS PLACE WASN'T for him. He had let that damn prick, Nicolaus Braun, get under his skin with his talk about this being Whiskey's neighborhood. All his bullshit about Whiskey having his reasons for sticking hard to Easton's case. The thing was— Nicolaus was righter than he knew. It did chap Whiskey's ass that Easton had been brutalized in this neighborhood. His turf. This area was a place where the GBLTQ community should feel safe to walk to their cars alone. He had worked the area for fifteen years. First as a beat cop and now as a detective. It was his responsibility to keep people safe. He had failed. Nicolaus implied Whiskey's responsibly went deeper—like he was a member of the community. That accusation was a little harder to swallow, but true nonetheless. Not that anyone knew. He came from the type of family that named him Whiskey, for God's sake. That was really all anyone needed to know to form a picture of the type of people they were.

For happiness' sake, and his sanity, Whiskey was trying to live more openly. It was possible he shouldn't have started here—in a bar filled with pretty boys who were all way too young for him. For fuck's sake. He'd been called Daddy at least six times by perfectly styled and—no doubt—hairless kids who looked no older than fourteen. While Whiskey was certain there were tons of men who liked that title, he wasn't one. Whiskey was an adult. He wanted an adult. Giving up, he chugged the last of his beer, tipped his bartender, and headed for the door. Whiskey almost made it. The exit was in sight. A solid and warm hand slid across his stomach. Expensive-smelling cologne overcame him. A deep voice and warm breath caressed the shell of his ear. "Do you truly intend to leave without letting me buy you a drink?"

Whiskey turned his head. His mind went blank. He wasn't exactly a silver fox. More of a salt and pepper hottie. He was the perfect combination of well-dressed, clean-shaven, and rough around the edges. Like he could be a CEO, but he would still change a tire. In the bad club lighting, Whiskey couldn't tell what color his eyes were, but the hard line of his jaw definitely had Whiskey's attention.

"I can make time for one more drink."

A smile so wicked it punched Whiskey in the gut touched the man's lips. With his hand still pressed to Whiskey's stomach, he motioned a nearby waitress closer. He spoke close to her ear. She nodded before heading to the bar. "She'll bring our drinks."

"You didn't ask what I want."

Whiskey had to take a breath at the confidence in the guy's stare. "Don't worry. I know what you want."

Damn. Whiskey was certain he did. His gaze dropped to the man's perfect lips. They were full and looked soft. "I'm Whiskey."

"Justice."

A smile exploded across Whiskey's face at the name. He liked that.

Justice's expression darkened with hunger as he stared at Whiskey. "Come. Sit." He steered Whiskey to a nearby table. Judging by the glass of dark liquor waiting, this was Justice's table. Whiskey had no clue how he had missed the man sitting there. The more he looked at Justice, the more his interest grew.

Damn, he was gorgeous—tall and trim. The light reflected Justice's eyes just right and Whiskey's breath caught. They were ice blue.

The waitress returned as Whiskey slid into the chair beside Justice. "Whiskey sour." Whiskey bit his bottom lip, trying to hide his smile. It was his favorite drink.

"Thank you."

Justice's lips touched the shell of Whiskey's ear again, making goosebumps race down his body. "I told you I know what you want."

Okay, seriously, Whiskey was interested. He refused to show it to someone he had just met. "What do you do, Justice?" Whiskey deliberately said Justice's name to feel how it rolled off his tongue. He liked the way it tasted.

Justice waited until Whiskey met his stare before answering. It was such a power move that Whiskey found he couldn't look away. "I'm vice president of the accounting division of a major corporation. What about you?"

Not a CEO but close. Whiskey's instincts had always been his strongest attribute. "I'm a detective for the Santa Clara county police department."

Justice's mouth lifted in one corner. He sipped his

drink, stealing his expression from Whiskey before he could get a read on Justice. By the time he set his glass aside, Justice's face was unreadable. He draped his arm across the back of Whiskey's chair. His thumb stroked Whiskey's shoulder. "What brings one of Santa Clara's finest into a place like this?"

Whiskey cast a quick look around. He wasn't sure how to take the question. It wasn't his type of place, but he didn't think Justice had any reason to think so. In the end, he shrugged. "I work this neighborhood. I've probably driven past this place a million times but never been inside. It was time to check it out, I suppose." It wasn't entirely comfortable beneath Justice's intense stare. Whiskey found himself sipping his drink to give himself something else to focus upon.

"You don't fit in here."

Whiskey's gaze swung back Justice's way. Justice didn't look judgmental. In fact, his serious expression hadn't wavered. "I know." Even Whiskey heard the defeat in his voice.

A subtle change passed over Justice's features. He leaned in again, speaking close to Whiskey's ear. "You're not twelve like everyone else here."

A burst of surprised laughter escaped Whiskey.

"God, they do all look like jailbait, don't they? This place makes me feel ancient."

A sardonic smile touched Justice's lips. "Imagine how I feel."

Whiskey eyed Justice for a second. He set his elbow on the table and turned in his seat, making a show of looking Justice over. "What brings you to a place like this?"

"A meeting with a potential client. I was finishing my drink after its conclusion when I spotted you. We should find something more fitting for adults to do."

A smile tugged at Whiskey's lips. "What do adults do? All I do is work."

Justice laughed. It was deep, rumbling, and hot. Whiskey found it a little harder to breathe all of a sudden. Justice's eyes swam with humor. "Finish your drink." Despite Justice's easy tone, there was no mistaking it was an order. Whiskey tossed back his drink without argument. It was worth it to see the hunger growing in Justice's gaze at his acquiescence. "Good boy. Now dance with me."

As if Justice was fate's master, a slow song came on. Whiskey decided to take it as a sign. He pushed the chair away from the table. "All right."

Justice set his hand on the small of Whiskey's

back and steered him toward the dance floor. Once they joined the rest of the bodies coming together, Justice pulled him close. It was warm and smelled good in Justice's arms. There was no awkwardness. Justice held him too close for Whiskey to think about the beat. He simply matched Justice's every move because he was incapable of moving away. Whiskey was too captivated by Justice's intensity. He watched Whiskey with so much open hunger that Whiskey expected to get torn apart. Oddly, Whiskey couldn't wait.

Somehow, Justice managed to hold Whiskey a little closer. Whiskey's body reacted without his permission. Justice's touch was commanding. Just the way Whiskey liked. Justice leaned in and brushed his lips across the spot beneath Whiskey's ear, making Whiskey's breath catch. "By the way, you know damn well what adults do."

Whiskey's insides twisted with lust and excitement. His heart skipped a beat. "I don't live that far from here." The words fell from Whiskey's lips before he knew he would make the offer. He regretted nothing.

Without another word, Justice took his hand and led him toward the door. Whiskey didn't look right or left. His gaze stayed locked on the way Justice's body moved—like a predator. Damn, it was possible he was making a huge mistake. He was so goddamn tired of being good. Whiskey wanted more. He wanted the passion he had seen when Nico stared at Easton. The kind of intensity that led Nico to kill for Easton. He felt empty without that level of insanity in his life. Justice would rock him to his soul. Whiskey felt it. Even if Justice only wanted him for one night, Whiskey would take it. He was so goddamn exhausted from being the responsible adult. Justice would fix that.

GOING HOME WITH WHISKEY HADN'T BEEN PART of Justice's plan. As he led Whiskey through the club and out the door, Justice told himself he was feeling things out as he went. He hadn't expected Whiskey. Justice liked studying people, learning their interests and weaknesses. Whiskey made that impossible. The man hadn't lied earlier. All he did was work. If he had any wants, hopes, dreams, or even hobbies, Justice hadn't seen it. All he had seen Whiskey do on his time off was poke at old cases. Cases better left alone.

Unfortunately for Justice, the moment Whiskey

chugged that drink upon order, Justice's every kink was engaged. He loved a man who obeyed. In that moment, his plans for the evening changed.

He didn't slow until he had the passenger side of his Mercedes open. Justice hauled Whiskey against him beside the open door. For a moment, he let Whiskey feel his desire. Whiskey stared at him with flushed cheeks and heat in his eyes. Justice's mouth went dry. "Get in." Justice had to take a breath when Whiskey immediately obeyed without question. Goddamn. That was hot. Justice circled the car and slid behind the wheel. "Address."

"1250 Wren Way."

With a nod, Justice headed that way. An inner battle raged. If he did this, Justice risked Whiskey walking away, satisfied by a single night together. If he didn't do this... Justice wasn't sure what would happen. All he knew was there was a tick in his jaw —like he hadn't stopped grinding his teeth since the moment he stopped Whiskey from leaving that club. He needed... something. Something more. Since Justice wasn't in the business of denying himself, they were doing this.

"I don't bring people home." Whiskey's claim snapped Justice from his inner raging. He cast a quick glance Whiskey's way. Whiskey stared straight ahead, looking tense as hell. "I don't go home with people either," he added, as if Justice might misinterpret his first claim.

"I wouldn't have accepted your suggestion if I thought you did." Justice swore he could feel Whiskey's unease growing. It filled the air, sucking up the oxygen in the car. He could feel his control slipping. Justice had to act before Whiskey changed his mind. He cleared his throat and tried hard to seem more human than he was. "This is unusual for me too, but I don't meet people often who make me laugh. I'm a bit," Justice searched for a good way to describe himself that wouldn't scare the hell out of Whiskey. "serious," he said finally, choosing something milder than the truth.

A low and sexy-sounding chuckle came from the passenger seat. Whiskey's hand slid up Justice's thigh, making his breath catch. "Serious or stern?"

Goddamn, he wanted Whiskey. Justice counted to three in his head while taking a slow breath. He let a smile touch his lips. "Both, I suppose. Where I'm from—" Justice damn near bit his tongue off as he realized what he had said. He backpedaled. "The house I grew up in was very... military, I suppose. We were always expected to show discipline. It's not something you outgrow."

Whiskey turned sideways in his seat. Justice could feel his stare. "You said 'we.' Do you have siblings?"

"Just one." Justice decided some honesty might go a long way. "A younger brother. What about you?" Because Justice had to stop talking about himself.

"I'm the youngest. I have two older brothers—Miller and Jack, and yes, they too are named after alcoholic beverages." The laughter in Whiskey's voice had Justice's smile turning genuine.

"I have to know."

"My parents are California implants," Whiskey answered, easily understanding his question. "They moved from the deep south to here a year after they were married. My dad was military too. Apparently, you can take a southerner from the south, but you can't beat the country out of them."

Justice pulled into Whiskey's driveway without thought. Too late, he recognized his ease at finding Whiskey's house could be suspect. Justice went with distraction to save himself. Without giving Whiskey time to guess at his intentions, Justice put the car in park, snagged Whiskey by the back of his neck, and hauled him in for a kiss. He didn't move slow or tease. Justice kissed Whiskey hard and deep. Even though Justice only meant to keep Whiskey unbalanced, he ended up being the one caught off guard. Whiskey immediately submitted to Justice, turning to jelly beneath Justice's attack. Justice fought the urge to climb across the car and take everything he wanted. Instead, he forced himself to slow. Their kiss softened. He barely stroked Whiskey's tongue with his. Justice pulled back a little more with every brush until their lips barely met. By the time he leaned away enough to see Whiskey's face, Whiskey looked dazed. Justice swiped his thumb along Whiskey's bottom lip, because he needed to feel it. "Maybe I should leave you right here. I don't want you to regret me."

Whiskey shook his head. "I'm not afraid."

That one statement punched Justice so hard, he couldn't breathe. Whiskey could have chosen anything to say. He could have sworn he wouldn't regret a thing. Said he was an adult who knew his mind. Instead, Whiskey wasn't afraid—like he saw the black void inside Justice where a soul should be, and he wanted Justice anyhow. The need to twist and control grew until Justice scared himself. Whiskey should be fucking terrified.

Justice unsnapped Whiskey's seat belt. "Lead the way."

WHISKEY COULD FEEL JUSTICE'S INTENSE GAZE upon him like a physical touch as he unlocked the front door of the duplex. Nervousness set in as they stepped inside. Judging by Justice's clothes and car, the guy had money. Whiskey did not. Not only was this a ridiculously expensive town to live in, he didn't make big bucks as a community servant.

"Sorry it isn't much," Whiskey said as he switched on the light. He tossed his keys onto the scratched up wooden coffee table. At least he had cleaned recently. That was the only thought Whiskey managed before Justice was in his space. Whiskey automatically met Justice halfway, as if they'd kissed a thousand times before. This kiss was different from the one in Justice's car. It was every bit as hungry, but there was patience mixed in. Promise. Justice wouldn't leave him unsatisfied. Whiskey didn't wait for him to make the first move. As their tongues stroked, Whiskey tugged Justice's shirt from his pants, untucking it. He fumbled for the buttons, starting from the bottom. Whiskey's clumsy fingers showed his nerves. The truth, he was more in the closet than he liked to admit. He had only been with two other men, and each one only once. Those had been quick, secretive tumbles that probably bordered on not being considered sex at all. He didn't bring men home. This was a lot. Between stepping inside that club, dancing with Justice, and now leaving his car behind to let Justice bring him home, Whiskey was two steps away from hyperventilating.

Whiskey managed three buttons before Justice stopped him. Justice's eyes looked hard as he pulled away. Whiskey's heart sank. Justice was probably used to more confident and experienced men. No doubt Whiskey's bumbling through everything was a turn-off.

"Take your shirt off."

Whiskey's heart skipped a beat. There was no denying it was an order and Justice expected to be obeyed. Whiskey might not have, but then Justice went to work on the buttons of his shirt. He nearly swallowed his tongue as the two halves of Justice's shirt fell open, revealing a chiseled torso covered in a huge tattoo. Whiskey immediately tugged his own shirt up and over his head, tossing it aside. There was no way he was taking a chance of Justice buttoning back up his shirt before Whiskey got a shot at seeing the entire picture. Justice let the shirt slip from his body.

"Goddamn." Whiskey couldn't stop the word from falling from his lips. The ink was a huge skull and roses. Never in a million years had Whiskey expected such a perfectly pressed man to be so different under his clothes.

Justice's lips twitched, as if he found Whiskey's reaction humorous but he tried hiding it. "I want the rest of your clothes gone." Justice crossed his arms over his chest. With his feet braced and his eyes locked on Whiskey, it was obvious he waited to be obeyed. In that moment, there was nothing Whiskey wouldn't have given Justice. His body ached. He burned. No one understood the torture of constantly denying himself, torn between expectation and reality.

His hands went to the button of his jeans. His fingers didn't fumble as they had done before. Justice's hard gaze steadied him. He stripped bare beneath Justice's watchful stare. The nervousness might have returned, but Justice looked starved—like Whiskey was the only thing that would assuage his hunger. It was empowering as hell.

"Beautiful." The one word of praise from Justice nearly took out Whiskey's knees. Whiskey had always considered himself average in every way. The way Justice eyed him had pride swelling in his chest.

Without a word, Justice moved to the plush chair Whiskey sat in each night, toed the footstool out of the way, and sat. Whiskey's gaze followed his every move. His back was covered in ink too. A dragon. The moment he was settled, Justice returned to watching him like a hawk. Whiskey was his prey. "Touch yourself."

He had never been on display like this for anyone. He palmed his cock, expecting awkwardness would set in at any moment. The lust was too thick for anything else. Ripples of pleasure ran down his erection as Whiskey stroked his dick the way he liked. One thing he had gotten very used to doing was pleasuring himself. He knew what he wanted, even if no one else seemed to understand. Whiskey pumped and squeezed tighter each time he reached his crown. Pre-cum soaked the tip. As he looked on, Justice leaned to the side and dug out his wallet. He pulled out a condom. Whiskey didn't even blink as he massaged his hard dick and watched Justice set his cock free. Fuck. He was perfect. Whiskey was torn right down the middle between wanting to come and needing more. Justice rolled the condom down his length. His gaze didn't waver from Whiskey, as if he needed Whiskey to understand the dick was for him. Whiskey felt the impact to his soul.

Justice was sexy as fuck and he was fully hard, and all of it was for Whiskey.

"Do you have lube?"

Whiskey gave a jerky nod at the question. His tongue didn't want to work.

"Get it."

Without question, he headed for the bedroom, following the order he had been given. Justice was in charge. Whiskey had one job—to please Justice. He snagged the small tube from the bedside and returned to his earlier spot.

Justice gave him a sharp nod. Whiskey swelled with even more pride beneath Justice's praise. "Lube your asshole. I want to watch."

A hint of discomfort tried sneaking in. They were so far out of Whiskey's comfort zone, he couldn't see the shore. But Whiskey was determined to see this through. He squeezed some lube from the tube before tossing the tube aside.

"You are so gorgeous."

There was something magical in Justice's praise. Whiskey was incapable of wussing out beneath it. He swiped the lube across his asshole. His body twitched, greedy for release.

"Come sit on Daddy's lap."

Oh, fuck. Pre-cum ran down his length at the

words. He had never been so goddamn turned on in his entire life. As much as he'd hated those boys calling him Daddy, he loved hearing Justice refer to himself in that light. His heartbeat pounded in his ears. He crossed the room, holding Justice's stare every step of the way. Whiskey straddled Justice's lap, facing him. He kept his weight braced on his knees and his balance by holding on to the back of the chair. Justice's hands ran up his thighs. Goosebumps rose on his skin. His cock jumped. Whiskey's entire body was lit like one big nerve. Justice didn't touch Whiskey's erection. Whiskey wondered if his brain would snap under the pressure of wanting and waiting. He had never been more tuned in to someone's touch. Justice's hand moved closer to where Whiskey wanted him. He held his breath. Justice's hands ran between Whiskey's thighs and crotch, coming inches from where Whiskey wanted to be touched the most. He stared down at Justice in desperation. Justice lightly brushed Whiskey's balls with one finger before moving lower.

Whiskey bit back a whimper. He felt needy as fuck. Even though he knew he could reach down and jerk off at any time, he wanted Justice's touch. Justice fingered the spot between Whiskey's balls and asshole. Madness scratched at Whiskey's brain.

"Please?" The desperate-sounding plea escaped Whiskey with no input from his brain. His body was ready to snap and he couldn't stand another second.

Justice struck without warning or mercy. He pushed upward at the same time as he forced Whiskey down, impaling Whiskey on his cock in one thrust. Pain sliced through him. Whiskey hadn't been prepared for it. Then Justice grabbed his dick, and nothing made sense anymore. He held tight and pumped fast while simultaneously rocking Whiskey on his cock. There was an internal bump that rolled his eyes back in his head while Justice worked magic on his dick. Whiskey tried to move. He wanted more.

"No," Justice barked, forcing him still. "I'm in charge here. Sit still—like a good boy. Trust me to give you everything you need. I'll make it better."

Whiskey was positive he couldn't take the madness, until Justice rocked again, massaging him internally. "Oh, God." Whiskey tried holding his tongue, but he couldn't. No amount of biting it would make his tongue stop. "Fuck, Justice. I want... I don't know."

"Shhh," Justice soothed, calming him. "I know." He sounded so calm and sure while Whiskey was certain he wouldn't be the same mentally after this. "I'll fix you." He let go of Whiskey's cock and grabbed his hips, tilting them at a different angle before surging upward again. Pressure and pleasure strained through Whiskey. He cried out, begging and needy. Justice repeated the same move. "Come for Daddy," Justice demanded as his dick punched that spot that felt so goddamn good. Whiskey lost his breath. Pleasure popped behind his eyes as an orgasm slammed into him. His cock danced and twitched, coating Justice in cum. He had never had an orgasm without direct contact to his dick. There was no denying Justice had done just that for Whiskey.

He held the back of the chair and rode out the waves. Justice gasped and shook beneath him, as if Whiskey's orgasm had triggered his. Whiskey was so blown away, he couldn't think straight enough to make sense of anything. He was lost. There was no low he wouldn't stoop to have this again. He'd never felt anything as powerful. Even if Justice only meant to have Whiskey for one night, Whiskey knew he couldn't go back to hiding after this. This was everything his life had been missing. He wanted more.

TWO

DAYLIGHT SLAMMED into Whiskey's eyes as he shot awake. It took Whiskey a minute to figure out why he felt out of sorts—like something was missing. Justice was gone. He settled back down, letting the pillows swallow him. The scent of Justice's expensive cologne overcame him. His head automatically turned, hunting for the smell. It was the pillow beside him. Whiskey shamelessly buried his face in the pillow and inhaled.

Whiskey tried keeping his mind blank. Something horrible lingered just on the other side of looking at things too closely. Images of the night they shared kept flashing through Whiskey's mind. They had moved to the bedroom where Justice had transformed from controlling to sweet. He'd kissed and stroked Justice for hours until he had finally succumbed to the exhaustion. Whiskey hugged the pillow tighter. He bit his lip, trying not to smile like an idiot at nothing.

His smile slipped away. Justice was gone. He had left without saying goodbye. Whiskey had feelings about that, but he couldn't go down that road. He pressed the pillow to his face one last time before rolling from the bed. His bladder was screaming at him for being lazy. He ran through his usual morning routine, but in the end, he put on pajama pants instead of getting dressed. Today seemed like the perfect day to do nothing at all.

Whiskey dragged his feet on the way to the kitchen. He needed coffee. *Don't think.* If Whiskey knew anything at all, he knew he couldn't let himself think. He had known going in that he was headed into a one-night stand. Justice was a stranger, yet Whiskey had brought him home fully intent on getting fucked. Normal people didn't wake up from flings feeling like this—lost and like a piece of him had gone missing.

He rubbed his chest. Fuck. He was such a sucker for love at heart. Maybe that was why he never dated. Whiskey's fingers froze on the handle of the refrigerator. A magnet from his favorite pizza joint held a note in place. A smile tugged at the corners of his mouth as he eyed Justice's strong signature at the bottom. He snagged the paper and read.

Whiskey,

Whiskey bit his bottom lip. Justice had spelled his name right. Most people left out the e.

I had an early morning appointment and had to run. You were sleeping too peacefully for me to disturb you. If you're interested, I'd love to make you dinner tonight. Text me and let me know a time, and I'll pick you up. If last night was all you were looking for, I won't look for your text. I'm leaving things in your court. By the way, I enjoyed meeting you. I never go home with anyone. You should text me. — Justice

Whiskey stared at the phone number scratched across the bottom of the note, fighting a smile. He was scared to hope. In his profession, Whiskey didn't meet nice people. He only dealt with the dregs of society. It was obvious Justice was doing well financially. He didn't need Whiskey for anything other than company. Fuck him. Whiskey recognized the pressure in his chest as hope. It was too late to pull back. Since there was no undoing last night, Whiskey headed back to the bedroom to get his phone. There was no time like the present to start the descent into possible heartache. What the hell. He only had one life to ruin.

Whiskey: *I wish you'd woken me. Dinner sounds nice. I'm off today, so whatever time works for you. Now I just need to find a way to get my car from Fusion's parking lot, lol.*

To Whiskey's surprise, Justice's response came seconds after Whiskey hit send.

Justice: *I had to drive by there this morning to get to work. There were two cars in the lot. A red Dodge Durango and a black Ford F-150. Which is yours?*

Whiskey: *The Ford.*

Justice: *I'll take care of it.*

For a moment, Whiskey stared at his phone in confusion. He didn't know what Justice meant. Whiskey shrugged. It was possible Justice planned to take him to get it later. That was fine. He didn't want to do anything. Whiskey couldn't recall the last time he felt this lazy. Plus, he sort of wanted to ruminate now that it was safe to think. This was more than a one-night stand.

Justice: *I'll be there at six.*

Whiskey: *I'll be waiting.*

With fucking bells on because meeting Justice was the best thing to happen to him in a long damn time.

THE DIGITAL RAINDROPS SLIPPING DOWN HIS computer screen blurred. Justice blinked and immediately zoned out again. Normally, the peace-inducing image calmed him. Today, Justice couldn't keep his inner demons at bay no matter what he tried. This was why he didn't touch people. Not sexually, anyhow. Inside, Justice was a dark hole. He was obsessive and controlling. Justice had thought Whiskey would be different. He had gone in with a clear methodical plan. Then, Whiskey's hot cum had coated Justice's chest and Whiskey had looked at Justice completely unguarded. Justice shook his head, trying to get the image from his head. Those light brown eyes and ridiculously long lashes, they wouldn't be dispelled from Justice's mind. Whiskey had looked at Justice as if no one had ever seen him before Justice—like he had been invisible until the moment he had straddled Justice's lap.

Justice's phone rang, distracting him from his increasingly obsessive thoughts. Whiskey's name flashed on the face of his phone. A smile that felt evil even to him pulled at Justice's lips. He pressed the device to his ear. "Hello?"

"How did you do it?"

Justice's smile grew to the point it could be heard in his voice. "Do what?"

"I just looked outside, and my truck is in the driveway. How in the hell did you manage that?"

Justice leaned back in his chair. Satisfaction raced through his veins. "A good magician never reveals his secrets."

Silence filled the air for a moment before a delicious rumble of laughter caressed Justice's ear. "Magician is a good description of you. At the risk of scaring you away, I'm ridiculously excited to see you later."

"Mhmm. Same." Justice didn't bother hiding the heat in his voice. He had plans for Whiskey. "Give me another hour to finish here, and I'll be there."

"I'm waiting."

Justice had to draw a slow breath at the heat in Whiskey's voice. He was so goddamn hot. Tall, dark, and muscular. Fuck. "Bye, sexy."

"Bye." The happiness in Whiskey's voice fucked with him a little. He had an hour. It was time to get moving. Justice picked up the gun on his desk and stood. He didn't have time to fuck around any longer. Justice had a job to finish.

No matter which direction Whiskey looked, he saw another reason Justice was way out of his league. Justice's house was amazing. The place wasn't obnoxious. It was Whiskey's version of perfect. The kitchen was definitely a cook's kitchen. It was huge and had every amenity any real chef would envy. Stools were built into the black marble island. All the appliances were stainless steel and a huge window lined the wall above the sink and counter, giving him a perfect view of the pool. Beyond the pool, the ocean. It seemed Whiskey had gone into the wrong business.

As lovely as the five-bedroom house was, the place was nothing compared to Justice. Unlike last night, when Justice had been dressed for work, tonight, he looked relaxed. Worn jeans and a black t-shirt molded to the world's sexiest body. Whiskey had a damn hard time swallowing his dinner around his lust. The thing was, Justice was also a fantastic cook. He had no idea how someone so flawless was single.

Justice grabbed a few things from the fridge and turned off the oven. "I hope you saved room for dessert."

Whiskey broke. "Jesus Christ. How has no one locked you down?"

Justice set a pot on the eye of the stove, throwing in items while openly avoiding making eye contact. He didn't answer right away. When he finally responded, Justice sounded hesitant. "I'm not for everyone."

"I guess that's a lucky thing for me then." At Whiskey's claim, Justice looked up from his task and gave Whiskey a heated glance before going back to work. Whiskey drew a slow breath. There was darkness inside Justice. Whiskey wanted to see more. "I smell the chocolate cake in the oven, but what else are you making?" Whiskey asked instead of jumping Justice. After all, as much as he wanted to touch Justice, he also wanted to know him.

"It's chocolate lava. Cake goes on the bottom. Then, vanilla ice cream." He pointed at the pot. "This is the chocolate syrup that goes on top. It all kind of melts together."

Even though he had just eaten a huge meal, Whiskey's mouth watered. An image of drizzling chocolate on Justice's nude body formed in Whiskey's mind. He had to take a breath. Justice glanced around, as if he had misplaced something.

A sheepish smile touched Justice's lips. "I forgot to bring the ice cream inside."

Whiskey waved off his words. "Don't worry over it. Point me in the right direction and I'll grab it."

Justice glanced around again, visibly trying to decide if he would let go of control for five seconds. That was one thing Whiskey already completely understood about Justice. He was always in charge. Obviously deciding his plate was already too full to do everything, Justice nodded. "All right. If you don't mind, it's in the freezer in the garage."

"I'm on it," Whiskey said, slipping from the stool. He stepped around the bar and headed for the door.

Before he made it, Justice stepped into his path. "Kiss me first." That was one request Whiskey could always fulfill. He brushed his lips across Justice's. He went back for more before finally moving away. Justice smacked his ass with the spatula as he passed. "Hurry back. This works best when the cake is still hot enough to melt the ice cream."

Whiskey jogged to the door. He had seen the chest freezer earlier and headed straight for it. The lid wouldn't lift. For a moment, confusion owned Whiskey. He took a step back and eyed the freezer. It had a huge dent in the side with a long scratch down the middle, but the damage didn't explain why the lid wouldn't lift. He tried again before it hit him.

Whiskey felt a bit stupid. It was locked. Whiskey cast a quick look around. There wasn't a key anywhere in sight. With an internal eye roll, he turned.

Justice stood in the open doorway, watching him. His expression was completely blank. It was odd. Justice almost seemed angry. He motioned to his left. "It's this one." Until the words left Justice, Whiskey hadn't noticed the tall freezer right by the door.

"Oh, sorry." He crossed the room. "That one was locked."

"It doesn't work," Justice said, watching his every move like a hawk. "I've got someone coming to haul it off tomorrow."

Whiskey flashed him a smile, hoping to lighten whatever mood had come over Justice. "If the chocolate sauce burns, you can blame me and my bad eyesight. I didn't even notice this one, and I had to walk right by it earlier to get inside." He opened the freezer door and Justice molded against Whiskey's back. His eyes fell closed as Justice's arms encircled him. Whiskey's chin hit his chest as Justice's lips brushed his nape.

"Were you insulting yourself? Is that what I just heard?"

Justice didn't sound angry, merely stern. "It was

a joke." Even to Whiskey's ears, he sounded breathless.

"I'm not so sure," Justice said as he slipped the button loose on Whiskey's jeans. "It sounded to me like you need to be taught a lesson."

Even while standing inside the open freezer door with cold air blasting him, Whiskey was on fire. He grabbed hold of the nearest shelf and held on for dear life as Justice shoved his hand inside Whiskey's jeans. Justice's teeth sank into the spot where Whiskey's neck met his shoulder. He ruthlessly massaged Whiskey's cock. Whiskey sucked air when his head spun. Justice had a way of taking Whiskey from zero to sixty in a heartbeat. Logically, Whiskey recognized part of the fire that raged inside him was the freedom Justice gave. His whole life, Whiskey had one foot in the closet and the other poised to jump back inside. Being with Justice was acceptance, and that was fucking hot. There was no shame here. Only pleasure.

Justice's other hand joined the party. He squeezed and pumped while massaging Whiskey's balls. Whiskey held on to the freezer and openly fucked Justice's hands. Justice bit, sucked, and licked Whiskey's neck while Whiskey gave him every bit of access and freedom he needed to do whatever he wanted. Nothing else mattered but the pressure climbing up his shaft. Whiskey strained to reach for the ecstasy Justice's hands offered. A cry ripped from Whiskey. Justice pumped fast, squeezing out every drop of cum as Whiskey thrust, riding his palm and twitching with delight. There was nothing but bliss in Justice's arms. His eyes burned as he fought the emotions swelling inside him. Whiskey wanted this. He wanted to hang on to whatever it was that grew bigger between them. More than anything, he needed Justice to want it too. They had to be more than a weekend fling. He had to make Justice feel.

"I don't think I've learned my lesson."

A soft chuckle brushed Whiskey's neck along with Justice's lips. "Is that so?"

Whiskey nodded. "I think you should let me lick you all over until I'm contrite."

Justice moved away. "Bring the ice cream."

At Justice's order, Whiskey grabbed the container of vanilla and followed Justice inside like being led by a tether. Whatever Justice had planned for the rest of the night, Whiskey was in. He had one thought stuck in his head like a mantra—Justice was his.

EVERY MUSCLE IN JUSTICE'S BODY ACHED AND turned to jelly. No one had ever left Justice such a mess. He wasn't as young as he used to be, but still. Whiskey blew his goddamn mind and wrecked his body. It was solely because he treated Justice like no other man had touched him before, as if no one else existed for him. It was addicting.

Justice kept brushing his fingers up and down Whiskey's back. He couldn't focus on anything except the bumps of Whiskey's spine. The softness of his skin. Whiskey's hand slid across Justice's stomach as he shifted, snuggling closer to Justice's chest—like he pressed closer to Justice's heartbeat.

"What are you doing tomorrow?"

A smile tugged at Justice's lips. He fought a chuckle, but it still sounded in his voice. "I'm guessing whatever you're about to ask me to do."

A tired-sounding chuckle rumbled from Whiskey as he kissed Justice's chest. "You might not want to agree before I ask. I have to go to a wedding."

Ugh. Whiskey was right. Justice shouldn't have agreed. Not that knowing changed anything. Justice would still go without argument. He brought Whiskey's hand to his lips. "That's fine." He kissed Whiskey's wrist at the pulse, letting his lips brush Whiskey's skin while he spoke. "Wear a suit. Sit quietly. It'll just be like any other day for me." He lightly licked Whiskey's wrist. "Except you'll be there, making everything worthwhile."

The way Whiskey watched Justice was the biggest power trip. Whiskey was strong. The only reason the man was powerless was because he had handed the reins to Justice. Whiskey was willing. Whatever Justice wanted, Whiskey would let him take it.

"Damn," Whiskey breathed, sounding mesmerized. "Tell me again why you're single."

"I'm not." Whiskey blinked, as if Justice threw cold water in his face. An evil smile pulled at Justice's lips. "I'm with you." He felt Whiskey melt and Justice knew he had won. Still, he couldn't let Whiskey misunderstand. "For the record, you're also with me. I don't share."

A soft chuckle vibrated from Whiskey. "You don't have anything to worry about."

Justice rolled, pinning Whiskey beneath him. The black hole that lived inside him that swallowed everything needed to be fed. Rage scratched at his brain. "Do you think I'm joking? You're mine."

Whiskey's smile slipped away, but the happiness didn't leave his eyes. "I know." His hands ran up Justice's back. "You're incredibly sexy when you turn possessive. I mean, you're always gorgeous, but when you're like this, you're irresistible."

He meant it. Justice felt the claim to his nonexistent soul. For whatever reason, Whiskey liked the darker side of Justice. The real version of him. Whiskey was totally fucked. He just didn't know it yet.

THREE

WHISKEY'S MUSCLES and lungs burned from abuse. Sand coated his legs, glued there by the sweat coating his skin. The sun beat down on his bare torso. He loved running on the beach. Even though he didn't live directly on the beach the way Justice did, he still ran every morning along the shore. Justice's close proximity was a convenience Whiskey would love to have every day. He would never have Justice's deep pockets, but he hadn't hesitated to take advantage of waking up in such a beautiful spot.

Justice had been sleeping when Whiskey slipped out for his run. As he neared the backside of Justice's house, he spotted Justice's muscular tattooed back in the pool. Whiskey picked up speed. He tried not to look too closely at the reason. Justice said they were a couple. Whiskey still hadn't recovered. Not really. He had never expected this. It was rare for Whiskey to be so lucky.

Whiskey slowed as he hit the stone walkway at the edge of the pool. Justice was on the phone. It took Whiskey a second to realize he spoke Russian. Perfectly. Accent and all. Whiskey didn't understand a word, but he recognized the language. Justice glanced over, catching sight of him. His gaze dropped to Whiskey's toes before slowly lifting, burning every spot he eyed with the fire in his gaze. He looked hungry.

With a sharp word, Justice set the phone aside. "Good morning, sexy."

A smile Whiskey couldn't control pulled at his lips. "Good morning. I didn't know you spoke Russian."

"I speak several languages. Did you enjoy your run?"

He guessed Justice didn't want to talk about this new discovery. That was fine. "Very much. Thank you. Did you enjoy your swim?"

Justice didn't smile. His stare remained heated. "Get in."

Whiskey glanced down at his sweat-coated skin and sandy legs. "I don't want to get your pool dirty."

"Get in." There was no mistaking it was an order.

With a sigh, Whiskey pulled his phone and wallet from his pockets and set them aside. He descended the steps. The water was ice cold compared to his overheated skin. At the bottom step, he hesitated. Justice snagged his waist and towed him in.

"Goddamn."

At his protest, Justice finally smiled. "You need cooling down. Not to mention, I've yet to get my morning kiss."

Whiskey decided to be as extra as possible. He wrapped his arms around Justice's neck, his legs around the man's waist, and claimed his mouth. Salt from the pool water coated Justice's lips. Whiskey wasn't deterred. He sucked Justice's bottom lip and tried licking the roof of his mouth. He teased until Justice's touch turned every bit as desperate. Justice palmed his ass, kneading and rocking Whiskey against his body. He always took Whiskey's breath.

Justice kissed a path to Whiskey's ear. He licked. "How long do we have until we need to leave for this wedding?"

It took Whiskey a moment to gather his thoughts with Justice touching him. "Um. It starts at one."

Justice loosened Whiskey's shorts like an expert. "I'll hurry."

Goddamn. Justice was a tornado that swept into Whiskey's life. Everything was different than it had been only days ago. He hoped Justice never stopped sweeping him away. The happiness growing inside him was unlike anything Whiskey had ever experienced. He wasn't sure if he could go back to being without Justice.

HALFWAY TO THE COUNTRY CLUB WHERE THIS wedding was being held, it occurred to Justice that he knew nothing about today's ceremony. All he knew was Whiskey had asked this of him. That was all that he had needed to know to agree. Whatever Whiskey wanted was his. Justice kept toying with Whiskey's fingers as he drove and lifting the man's hand to his mouth to kiss. He had no idea what was happening with him. Justice was not one to show affection to anyone. He told himself it was part of the plan. Justice knew the truth. He had no plan any longer.

"Whose wedding is this, anyhow? Friends or family?"

A soft chuckle rumbled from Whiskey's side of the car. "Neither. It's a weird story, actually."

"All right." Justice dragged out the words, showing his confusion.

"I worked this guy's case," Whiskey explained. "It was one of the worst attacks I've seen where the victim lived. He'd been walking to his car when a van pulled up and three men dragged him inside. After hours of every horror imaginable, they dumped him in the back parking lot of a popular nightclub. That was where a local business owner found him. In a twist of fate, they fell in love, and they're getting married."

Fuck. His. Life. Justice knew this story. Very well. He cleared his throat, trying to come up with an excuse to turn around. Justice had nothing. "And you're going to their wedding because...?"

"In truth, I wasn't given a choice."

Justice glanced over with raised eyebrows. Whiskey was smiling. That was the only reason Justice hid his temper spike.

"It's no big deal," Whiskey said, soothing his ire. "Actually, I really like Easton. He persevered and came out better. Now he owns his own business, and he's getting married. They're in love. I don't usually get to see this part of the cases I work. Actually, in my job, there's not typically a happy ending. Only grieving families. This is nice." Whiskey sounded like he was trying to convince himself more than Justice.

Justice kissed Whiskey's hand again. He would sit in the back and try not to be seen. The country club came into sight. It was a huge place and everything Justice expected. Growing up, he didn't know places like this existed. There was never a day he expected to be joining the line for valet parking in his one-hundred-thousand-dollar car. He was willing to bet no one else sitting in line had fought to be here the way he had. No doubt their money was as dirty, though.

The huge white building gleamed in the sunlight. It was unnaturally clean. A rainbow of color surrounded the building. Flowers of every variety. Truly, the place was gorgeous. Justice kept his hard shell in place to hide the way he didn't fit in. On the outside, Justice was everyone's equal. Inside, he was still the street fighter he had always been.

Justice slipped from the car, straightening his jacket. He tried focusing on anything but his surroundings. Whiskey waited for him to circle the car. Their fingers linked on the way to the door.

Whiskey ended up being the one who broke. "I feel like a pleather couch on a millionaire's porch."

A snort escaped Justice. Once the sound was out there, his walls came down. A loud laugh sneaked out. Several heads and disapproving sneers turned their way. Justice swiped at his eyes. He glanced Whiskey's way. He was smiling. "You're worth more than everyone in this place combined. Money doesn't buy class. Trust me." He brought Whiskey's hand to his mouth. "Fuck all these people."

A sweet smile touched Whiskey's lips. Possessiveness swelled in Justice's chest. He wouldn't stop doing everything in his power to make this man happy. Whiskey was his now.

"I guess we'd better find the garden room."

Justice nodded. "I suppose we should." He cast another look around, expecting to be forced to ask for help. Instead, he caught sight of a gold sign, pointing toward the garden room. "There," he said, nodding toward the sign. As one, they headed inside. It was small. There was no way he would avoid being seen. Justice suppressed a groan. Since there was nothing for it, he let Whiskey choose their seats. He chose a spot to the left near the front. Justice amused himself by people-watching. There weren't many people there. In fact, none of Nico's people had shown.

Justice would have expected as much if he had known whose wedding he was set to attend today. Nicolaus Braun was a seven-time heavyweight boxing champion. He had come to the States via the same route as Justice—with his fists and a will to be more. Sacrifices were always made in those situations. Nicolaus had left his family behind, running for his life from people who took more than they ever gave. Justice had run toward his only family, leaving his friends behind to rot in the pile of shit his and his brother's blood had saved him from. Neither Nico nor Justice regretted a thing. That did leave an empty room at a wedding, though. Justice didn't know why Easton didn't have many people there either. There were fifteen or sixteen people, tops. Four couples and the guys who worked at Nico's shop. Someone who looked like a reporter. Probably for some sports magazine or channel. Justice draped his arm across the back of Whiskey's chair and settled in. Whiskey's cologne tickled his nose. He moved closer to the scent. Without thought, his lips brushed the shell of Whiskey's ear. Whiskey set his palm on Justice's thigh and rubbed. Something shifted in Justice's chest. He hadn't meant to get attached. In fact, Justice hadn't thought he was capable of caring about anyone. Most of the time, Justice mimicked emotions. That is, when he bothered. Normally, he didn't give a damn if anyone thought he was human. Whiskey was different. He was special.

The room fell silent. Everyone turned in their seats. Justice glanced behind him. Going completely by their own guidelines, Nico walked with Easton down the aisle. Justice smiled at the idea of the couple making up the rules as they went. No one deserved happiness more. They wore matching white tuxedo jackets with black pants. Easton carried pink roses. They ignored everyone but each other as they made their way to the front. Their smiles spoke volumes. Things moved fast. It seemed one moment they were making their way toward the waiting Reverend. The next, they were giving their guests one hell of a PDA. They were adorable.

Before Justice could convince Whiskey to make a run for it, Easton cut them off, towing Nico in his wake.

"Whiskey Harris. I know you're not planning on running out without speaking to me."

They drew up short. "Of course not," Whiskey said, accepting Easton's hug. He shook Nico's hand. Justice tucked Whiskey against his side.

Nico's gaze slid Justice's way. Surprise crossed

his feature. He openly held Easton a little tighter to his side, as if he expected Justice's presence would ruin his life. Justice knew Nico had questions. It was the most important day of Nico's life. Justice did his best to set him at ease. He held his hand out to shake. "Justice Alexander. Thanks for letting me crash your wedding."

Nico accepted his handshake. "Nicolaus. This is my husband, Easton." He smiled as he said the words, making Justice realize he was the first person Nico had been allowed to say that to.

"I've seen you fight," he said before turning his attention Easton's way. Because he knew Easton's story, Justice intentionally softened as he shook the man's hand. "It's lovely to meet you both." Justice went back to holding Whiskey's waist, making it known he was only there for one reason—Whiskey.

Easton's green eyes flashed with happiness. He looked thrilled to be married to Nico. That warmed Justice's dead heart. "I can't tell you how much I appreciate you coming. Neither of us had many people who could attend."

"What am I?" Whiskey asked, opening his arms to Easton again. "Does my presence not count?" he added as he hugged Easton.

"You're a friend," Easton said, hugging him back.

"You're required to be here by the friendship bylaws."

Whiskey looked a bit taken aback by Easton's claim—like he hadn't realized they were friends. His expression shifted just as quickly, hiding his reaction before Easton saw. He shook Nico's hand. "Congratulations. You won the lottery."

"This is true. I'm not worthy, but I try."

Easton lightly smacked Nico on the stomach, but he looked happy. Justice felt a spurt of pride on Nico's behalf. He'd won. Maybe the man had a shit family and an even shittier past, but Nico had met the sun and won him. That was not something that happened often with men such as them. Without thought, Justice's gaze slid Whiskey's way. He shouldn't look at Whiskey in the same light Nico saw Easton. This was not a love affair. Whiskey's gaze slid his way as he listened to Easton chatter happily. Justice couldn't look away from the humor shining in Whiskey's eyes. A wave of unexpected longing crashed over Justice. They weren't the same as Nico and Easton, he reminded himself again. But Whiskey was his. One hundred percent. Justice would kill anyone who touched him.

"You're being awful quiet." Whiskey kissed Justice's throat as he made the claim, because he couldn't stop. It was ridiculous how weddings always hit him hard. Made him dream. It did not help that Justice had brought him home after the wedding and hadn't stopped cuddling with him all day.

A delicious smile touched Justice's lips. "I'm always quiet." He kissed Whiskey's forehead. "For you, though, we can talk about whatever you'd like."

Whiskey went back to staring at the ocean from the lounge chair by the pool. He snuggled closer to Justice's warmth. "It's cool. I was just making sure you're okay."

Justice brought Whiskey's hand to his mouth, something he had noticed Justice liked doing. He pressed his lips to Whiskey's palm. "I like you a lot."

The confession surprised Whiskey. Justice didn't seem the type to talk about feelings. "I like you a lot too."

"Will you stay with me again tonight, if I promise to get you home in time for work?"

Whiskey swore even his heart smiled. "I'd love that."

With a nod, Justice pressed Whiskey's hand to his heart and went back to staring at the horizon. "I spend a lot of time alone. That's why I'm quiet. It's

47

not that I have nothing to say. I'm just not very exciting."

"I disagree," Whiskey argued. "I haven't stopped being excited since we met." A low chuckle left him. "That came out wrong. I didn't mean that sexually, even though that's true too and I realize how my words sounded." He took a breath when he realized he was rambling. "I meant I haven't had so much to look forward to in a long time. You make me excited to see what happens next. Do you have an accepting family?" Whiskey had to change the subject. Even to his ears he was beginning to sound pathetic.

"I have no family."

Confusion rocked Whiskey. He leaned away to meet Justice's stare. "Wait. I thought you said you have a brother."

Justice didn't respond right away. With his brow furrowed, he seemed muse over Whiskey's words before his face finally cleared. "Sorry. I do have a family. Everyone does. I meant I have no living relatives. My brother died several years ago."

"Oh." Whiskey settled back down, cuddling close to Justice. "That's sad. How old was he?"

"He was young. Could we talk about something else?"

Whiskey felt like shit for pushing. If all his

family was gone, he probably wouldn't want to talk about it either. "Of course. Sorry." Except, Whiskey couldn't think of anything to say. He had already stepped on Justice's toes.

Before Whiskey could think of a way to turn things around, Justice shifted positions. Whiskey found himself with a very sexy Justice straddling his lap. "I'm not trying to keep you from getting close. You don't have to walk on eggshells. I'll tell you anything you want to know. My birthday is April sixth. I'm fifty-one. Every morning, I get up and swim laps for an hour before going to a very boring job. All my suits are plain. I like my coffee black. Truth be told, I'm pretty rigid and I have no idea what you see in me. I also imagine you'll get bored before too long."

He was unhappy. That was what Whiskey really heard in that speech. Justice wasn't boring. He was existing. Whiskey was the same. He lived life on autopilot, doing the same things every day, getting by until... death, he supposed. Then, he had met Justice. Nothing had changed, except now he didn't want to do the same boring routine alone.

"Maybe all of that sounds nice to me—like you're steady. I won't wake up tomorrow and realize I turned my life upside down for someone who only sees me as a quick stop on the way to someone else."

A line appeared between Justice's brows. "Do you feel like I turned your life upside down?"

Whiskey wondered if he should be honest. Maybe Justice would decide Whiskey was too much drama. In the end, Whiskey knew it was best to find out now. "No one knows I'm gay. Not really—like I haven't actually said the words to anyone." He squeezed Justice's thighs as he spoke. His heartbeat pounded in his ears. He didn't want to lose Justice. "I mean, I guess some people know, but I've never confirmed their suspicions. But I don't care if people know I'm with you. I guess that's what I meant. Being with you will surprise some people in my life."

It felt like an eternity passed while Justice stared at him in silence. His expression gave nothing away. "You still haven't told me your birthday."

Relief poured through Whiskey. "It's September thirtieth. I'm thirty-five." Whiskey smiled, incapable of hiding his happiness. "Every morning, I get up and go for a run on the beach before going to a job I might not come home from. I see the lowest of society each and every day. It's left me disillusioned and bitter. I like my coffee sweet. You'll probably get sick of me working all the time. I can be a bit obsessive. Meeting you is the best thing that's happened to me in a really long time. I'm scared shitless I'll fuck this up."

Justice leaned in, holding Whiskey's stare the whole time. "You have nothing to worry about." Their lips met and clung. Justice changed angles. "I'm already addicted to you."

Whiskey's heart soared at the confession. Justice had no idea. Whiskey had never been more enamored by anyone or anything in his life. He would do anything to hang on to this.

FOUR

THE SUN BEAT down on Whiskey's skin, making it prickle like needles stabbed his shoulders and arms. He wasn't breathing hard yet. Neither was Whiskey pushing himself this morning. He was in the mood to take it easy. His mind was elsewhere. It was still lounging in bed with Justice, even though Justice had left for work early this morning and Whiskey had started out late. Some days, it was harder than others to leave behind the delectable man who had been living beneath Whiskey's skin for the last few months. Today, Whiskey fought hard with himself. Justice was becoming a sickness. Whiskey didn't have to work today. He wanted to spend every second with Justice. So much so, it felt like punishment that he couldn't.

Flashing lights in the distance caught Whiskey's eye. He picked up his pace. A crowd gathered around yellow crime scene tape. Leo Humphrey, another detective in a different department, stood out from the crowd, mostly because of his bald head and ridiculous height.

Whiskey dug out his wallet and flashed his badge as he neared the edge of the scene. If Leo was here, things were under control, but Whiskey had always been a nosy bastard. That was why he was good at his job.

"Hey, Leo," Whiskey called out, snagging the detective's attention.

A sunglasses-covered gaze swung his way. "Whiskey." He dropped his chin, openly eyeing Whiskey's bare chest and shorts over the top of his glasses. "Do you live close to here?"

Whiskey shook his head. His gaze moved to the mess they were trying to hide with sheets and police presence. A large white chest-style freezer sat open. It had a huge dent in the side with a scratch down the center. Whiskey was too far away to see what was inside, but he had his suspicions. He nodded toward the freezer. "What's going on?" he asked, ignoring Leo's question.

Leo waved him over. "Some local divers found

this when they took some tourists out on a dive. They marked its location and pulled it out later."

Whiskey glanced inside. Wrapped in thick plastic that had done nothing to save him from the water damage was a very dead guy. At least, Whiskey thought it was a guy. Being submerged hadn't done him any favors. Something about the freezer niggled at the back of his mind. "I'm guessing there's no hope for prints or any evidence, really."

Leo shook his head. "Nope. I imagine everything of importance washed away. We have an ID, though. Strangely, he still had his wallet." Leo held up a plastic evidence bag. "Stanley Bingham. A convicted pedophile released early on a technicality. We've been looking for him on a set of new charges. Guess we found him."

"Well," Whiskey said, biting his tongue before he finished his thought. The guy had gotten what he deserved.

"Ended up right where he belongs, if you ask me," Leo said, taking the words from Whiskey's mouth.

With his hands on his hips, Whiskey scanned the horizon, taking in the local businesses and the chest's proximity to certain places. "Still, this is Kapra territory. I should probably make a visit to the casino, turn up the pressure on the local mafia, and let them know what we've found."

Leo glanced around too, as if confirming Whiskey's thoughts. "That's probably a good idea. You won't learn anything, of course, but it's always good to let them know we're still around."

"Sounds good." For a moment, Whiskey eyed the freezer again. Fuck. It looked exactly like the one that had been in Justice's garage. All chest freezers looked alike, he reminded himself. With a shake of his head, Whiskey headed back, jogging at a faster pace. He couldn't spend the day with Justice, so he may as well work. It had been a long time since he had let the Kapra family know the police still worked the town Zander Kapra owned. Even if no one gave a damn about a dead pervert.

Whiskey cleared the patio door. Cold air brushed over his skin. Justice's house felt empty as hell without Justice's overwhelming presence. Sometimes he was blown away by how much Justice trusted him. He never hesitated leaving Whiskey alone in his home on Whiskey's days off. In truth, Whiskey rarely went home anymore. Justice hadn't asked him to move in and Whiskey hadn't given up his tiny duplex. Sometimes he drove himself crazy wondering where they were headed. Other times, he lived in the moment—thankful as hell to have any piece of Justice's life.

Whiskey ran through his shower and threw on the first clothes he came across. Technically, it was still his day off. He would keep things as casual as possible. After all, Kapra hadn't done anything wrong, as far as he knew. It wasn't until Whiskey climbed behind the wheel of his truck that his gaze slid toward the spot where the chest freezer once sat. Whiskey shook his head. He was being ridiculous. There was no way in hell Justice had ever killed anyone in his life. Sometimes, Whiskey wondered if he had been a cop too long.

HAVING HIS BOSS ZANDER'S BODYGUARDS, PYTOR and Yaro, up his ass all day while Zander lounged in bed with his gorgeous husband was just part of the job some days. Today, it was a bit on Justice's nerves. His irritation had nothing to do with Pytor and Yaro per se. The gigantic Russians were great at their job. Justice was just having one of those days where his skin felt too tight. He had left Whiskey behind, nude and sleeping, to come here and do nothing. Justice wanted to go home. He missed his sexy man.

Fuck. Whiskey was under his skin. All Justice wanted to do was be with him. He had long past forgotten why they had ended up together. Whiskey was his. That was all that mattered. He'd hoped to keep Whiskey too busy to bother with old cases on his days off. He had definitely accomplished that. Justice had lost himself too somewhere along the way.

The phone on his desk lit. Zander's receptionist's voice filled the air. "Mr. Alexander, there's a man here to see Mr. Kapra. He's refusing to accept that Mr. Kapra is indisposed."

Justice pinched the spot between his eyes where a pain bloomed. "I'll take care of it."

"Thank you."

While suppressing a sigh, he met Pytor's gaze. "Shall we?"

Pytor dipped his chin and opened the door for Justice. He led the way, shielding Justice in case it was some crazy guy with a grudge. Yaro moved from his post outside the door and fell into step behind Justice. Justice looked down at himself as he crossed the threshold of the front office. He straightened his shirt where it had come untucked a hair. Pytor stepped aside, obviously having assessed the situation and found no issues.

Justice looked up. "I'm—" He froze. Justice blinked at the sight of Whiskey. "Whiskey?"

"Justice." Whiskey didn't sound surprised. In truth, he sounded resigned. That couldn't be good.

Justice crossed the room, determined to brazen this out. "I... this is a surprise." He smiled. "A good one, of course, but I wasn't expecting to see you. What brings you by?"

Whiskey shook his head, as if shaking off some spell. A smile touched his lips. "Happy accident, I suppose. I came by to ask Zander Kapra some questions. This is..." He cleared his throat "... what are you doing here?"

"This is where I work. I thought you knew that," Justice explained as he leaned in and brushed his lips across Whiskey's. Whiskey let it happen. Justice took it as a good sign.

The shock hadn't quite left Whiskey's features. "I never thought to ask exactly where you work. I guess I somewhat assumed you worked for a big firm or whatever." Whiskey's gaze slid over Justice's shoulder where Pytor still stood guard. "But it's possible you told me, and I forgot."

Justice knew he had to distract Whiskey immediately. He linked fingers with Whiskey. "Come on, handsome. I'll show you my office."

Whiskey gave him a jerky nod but allowed Justice to lead him away. As they passed Pytor, Justice met his stare and gave the man a subtle shake of his head, letting him know not to follow. It was bad enough he had to explain working for the mob. The moment he had them inside his office and shut away from the world, Justice was in Whiskey's space. He held the man's hips and shuffled close. "You have no idea how happy I am to see you. I was just thinking about you. It's like I conjured you." He moved in for a kiss.

Whiskey dodged him. It was a punch in the throat. "I'm on duty."

Justice took a step back. The mask he wore for the world fell back into place. He released Whiskey and turned his back on him, heading for his desk. "Of course. What brings you by, Detective Harris?"

"Fuck." The one growled word was all the warning Justice got before he found himself hauled backward into Whiskey's arms. His back hit Whiskey's chest. Whiskey's lips brushed his ear. "I'm sorry. Seeing you here caught me off guard." His lips moved lower, skimming Justice's neck. "Damn. You always smell so fucking good. I've been thinking about you too."

Whiskey was a muscular guy. He had never tried using his strength to manhandle Justice before.

Justice never expected to find it so hot. He was not the submissive sort. Justice turned in Whiskey's arms, taking back his power. He claimed Whiskey's mouth, kissing him hard and deep. Punishing him. He didn't stop until he felt Whiskey melt.

When Justice pulled away, he held on to Whiskey's face. "Don't ever try denying me again, understood?"

Whiskey looked dazed, but he nodded. "Understood."

"Kiss me again and then I'll hear your questions for Zander."

"How about another kiss and lunch instead? I'm afraid my questions are work related and I can only talk with Zander."

"That sounds ominous, but I understand." Fuck. So much was going wrong today. He palmed Whiskey's hips and towed him closer. "You have an important job. I get that you have to shut me out sometimes."

Whiskey winced. His hands slid up Justice's chest to his shoulders before linking behind Justice's neck. He was so beautiful. An unexpected emotion hit Justice. One that he never experienced—guilt. He wanted them to be a team. Justice didn't want to hide anything from Whiskey.

"That didn't come out the way I meant. Can we go back ten minutes and pretend you came to have lunch with me?"

Whiskey kissed Justice's chin. "I missed you and thought I'd stop by and take you to lunch. Nothing makes me happier than showing off my sexy man."

At Whiskey's willingness to let things go and play along, Justice had never been hungrier. His appetite had nothing to do with food. A thought hit him. "Wait. I thought you didn't have to work today."

"Honestly, I don't. Something happened, and I decided to follow a lead. It can wait, though. I'd rather be with you."

Whiskey had no idea how much hope Justice derived from that statement. There was a chance Whiskey would choose him over everything. Justice needed that. His possessiveness skyrocketed at the thought. Without giving Whiskey a chance to deny him, Justice popped the button on Whiskey's jeans. A bark of laughter escaped Whiskey at the move.

"You're working."

"You're right," Justice said, keeping his tone as innocent as possible. "I'm working on my favorite project, keeping my man happy."

Whiskey's smile was everything. He looked like

the happiest man on earth. "I'm already ecstatic because I have you."

Justice took on his fakest disappointed tone. "Well, I mean, if you don't want me to put your dick in my mouth, I can't force you."

Whiskey turned serious in a flash. He touched Justice's jaw. His thumb stroked Justice's bottom lip. He looked... like a man in love. Justice's heart skipped a beat at the thought. His mouth went dry. There was nothing Justice wanted more, and he couldn't lie to himself about it.

Whiskey dragged Justice's bottom lip down with his thumb. His gaze stayed locked on Justice's mouth. "I wish you understood how much I want to spend every second with you." His gaze lifted. Justice was floored by the intensity of Whiskey's stare. "You mean everything to me."

Justice loved him. It hit him like a semi. Justice hadn't thought himself capable of love. Yet, here he was, staring at the only person to ever find his heart to touch it. While holding Whiskey's gaze, Justice kissed Whiskey's thumb. Whiskey's lips parted on a breath—like Justice stole the air from his lungs. Justice didn't look away. He needed Whiskey to see his honesty. Justice wasn't the type to hold back. "I love you."

Justice heard the breath catch in Whiskey's throat. "Jesus. What did I do to deserve you?" Whiskey sounded like the question had been meant for himself. Justice wondered if he would explode while waiting for Whiskey to process. "I love you too."

The final word barely finished passing Whiskey's lips before Justice sprang. He claimed Whiskey's mouth, needing to taste the confession on Whiskey's tongue. In that moment, Justice would have walked away from everything for Whiskey. All Whiskey needed to do was ask.

WITH THE SHOCK OF JUSTICE'S *I LOVE YOU* wearing off, Whiskey's discomfort over Justice's job slowly crept back in. In the heat of the moment, with happiness and endorphins running high, Justice had grabbed his laptop, proclaimed he could work from home, and swept Whiskey away. Now, with silence filling the room and nothing for Whiskey to do but stare at Justice, reality set in. Justice worked for Zander Kapra. Zander owned this town. Truthfully, he owned the entire west coast plus Vegas. Everyone knew. It just wasn't really talked about. But Whiskey was a cop. As far as he knew, no one had ever been able to tie Zander's name to anything illegal. His predecessor, the Conti; they'd had tons and tons of evidence on that bastard. Yet he still always managed to stay out of jail. Money bought a lot more than most people realized. Since his death, Whiskey had kept a close watch on Zander. He had suspicions about a few things but zero evidence Zander did anything outside the letter of the law at all. But now, Whiskey didn't know what to think.

Justice stared at his laptop, scowling. Whiskey stared at him. He was in love with this amazing man, and he was scared shitless he didn't know Justice at all. Whiskey couldn't stop himself from digging. There was something not right, and years of detective work pushed him over the edge into downright suspicious.

"Hey, who did you get to haul off that old freezer in the garage?"

Justice cast him a quick look. "A guy from work has a son who refurbishes old appliances and then sells them cheap. I let him have it."

"Oh, that's good. Kind of like recycling. Do you recall the son's name?"

Justice stopped what he was doing and focused on Whiskey. "Rob or something like that. Why?"

Whiskey tried looking as innocent as possible. "Just making conversation. There's a guy at work who has the worst luck with appliances. Something is always going out around his house. He mentioned needing a freezer. Knowing someone who sells them used could be a help."

Justice nodded. "I'll see if I can get a card or something for his store."

Whiskey smiled. "Thanks. That would be great." He was being ridiculous. There were millions of chest-style freezers in the world. Finding out Justice worked for Zander Kapra was messing with him more than he liked. Whiskey shook his head. He needed to learn to leave work at work. Not everyone hid some huge secret.

"You're bored."

Whiskey snapped back to reality at Justice's comment. "I'm not bored. I'm with you."

Justice shut the lid on his laptop. "Work can wait. I can't have my angel getting tired of being with me. What would you like to do?"

Guilt ate at Whiskey. He'd made Justice think he was unhappy, with his bullshit thoughts. "I want to sit here with you while you finish working. Being with you is never boring to me."

Justice visibly swallowed a sigh. "That's enough

of that. We should go to your house and start moving your things here. Don't you think?"

Whiskey blinked. "Um."

Justice's eyebrows rose.

A wave of happiness washed over Whiskey. Justice was serious. "Okay."

A smile exploded across Justice's face and Whiskey was lost. There was nothing he wouldn't do to see that smile. Justice stood and moved to stand over Whiskey. Whiskey leaned his head back against the couch and stared up at the man who owned him. Without a word, Justice dropped to his knees between Whiskey's feet. His hands slid up Whiskey's thighs. Justice's gaze never wavered from holding Whiskey's stare.

"You get that you're the most important piece of my life, right?"

Whiskey swallowed. Justice was always intense. This was different. Justice wasn't just saying words. He was asking Whiskey to hear him. "Yes."

"Good." Justice's gaze dropped. He watched his hands as they slipped the button loose on Whiskey's jeans and slid the zipper down. Whiskey's heart sped. His breathing shallowed. Justice looked cold and hard. It was hot as hell—like Whiskey was about to be methodically pleasured. His dick hardened.

Justice urged Whiskey to lift his hips. He peeled Whiskey's pants and underwear down his thighs. Justice kept his gaze locked on his task as he stripped away the bottom half of Whiskey's clothing. Whiskey slid lower as Justice pushed his knees apart. Justice lowered his head and kissed Whiskey's inner thigh. With his lips pressed to Whiskey's skin, Justice inhaled. Goosebumps skirted across Whiskey's skin. Justice moved higher, kissing a path to where Whiskey wanted him the most. Justice took his time, kissing everywhere but Whiskey's hot zones. Whiskey was openly panting. His cock jerked and leaked, needing Justice, but Justice had patience and discipline—like he had led the Spanish Inquisition. Justice's gaze flipped upward. His beautiful ice-blue eyes locked on to Whiskey. Whiskey bit back a whimper. He was lost. This man owned him. Whiskey had signed away the title to himself the first time he had let Justice touch him. There was no going back or getting out. Moving in with Justice was nothing. Whiskey would give Justice his soul without question.

A cry tore from Whiskey's throat as his crown finally scraped the roof of Justice's mouth. Everything else disappeared. He tossed every care away and accepted the truth. It didn't matter that

Justice worked for Zander. Whiskey wasn't sure it even mattered if Justice had stuffed that body in that freezer. Right here and now, being with Justice was the only thing that mattered to Whiskey. No one else existed for him.

FIVE

THE MALL WAS FUCKING PACKED. It was like no one worked anymore. Whiskey swore he used to be able to stop by any store during the day and it would be dead. Nowadays, everything was busy all the time. Maybe he was just getting old and cranky. Whatever the reason, Whiskey wasn't loving it. This trip was about Justice, though. That was all that mattered to Whiskey.

He stared at the gold ring he'd just purchased. Fuck him. Was he really going to do this? Maybe not today, but soon. For the first time in his life, he was completely certain about everything. Whiskey had zero doubts about his relationship with Justice. They were the real thing. He had spent the past week thinking about Justice working as an accountant for

Luna Hotel and Casinos. That was a huge job and important. Just because every location was owned by Zander Kapra, that shouldn't reflect on Justice. Luna was still a legitimate business. Justice had to be one hell of an accountant to land that gig. Whiskey should be proud. His man was totally awesome. Whiskey wanted to lock him down for good before someone better snatched Justice away.

With his gaze locked on Justice's gift, Whiskey was slow on the uptake when the first shot rang out. Then, the world exploded into panic. People scattered. Screams filled the air. More shots filled the air. As everyone ran for the doors, Whiskey crammed the ring in his pocket and pulled his gun from its holster. He headed toward the gunfire. The crowd parted like the sea, running in the opposite direction. Even in the heat of the moment, Whiskey ensured the badge on his belt was visible. The last thing he wanted was to make the crowd panic and reverse course, heading back into the line of fire. Following the sound of screams, Whiskey quickly peeked around the corner. There were people on the floor bleeding but no sign of a gunman. Whiskey leapt around the corner and crab-ran to the nearest victim. They were gone. It was a clean shot to the head. There was nothing Whiskey could do for the woman. He moved to the next. The dark-haired man shook and gasped for air. It didn't look like he had long.

Whiskey grabbed his radio from the back of his belt and called for help. More shots filled the air, closer than he expected. His side caught fire. Whiskey glanced down and saw blood. His heartbeat pounded in his ears. Everything slowed to a crawl. He had time for a thousand thoughts. One stood out from all the rest. He couldn't die today. Whiskey needed more time with Justice. He had to live so he could ask Justice to marry him. That was Whiskey's biggest dream now. He had to live long enough to see it come true.

JUSTICE WAS RESTLESS TODAY. HE COULDN'T explain why. There was a nervous flutter in his gut—like something bad was about to happen. Moving Whiskey in with him had been a huge risk. The closer Whiskey got, the more Justice had to hide. Not only was Whiskey worth it, Justice hoped Whiskey would accept him some day—warts and all. The only chance Justice had of that happening was if he imbedded himself so deep in Whiskey's life that

Whiskey couldn't get away. Otherwise, there was nothing about Justice that was good enough to keep.

"Pytor tells me that we had a visit from Detective Harris while I was working from home."

Justice suppressed a snort as he focused on Zander. Working from home. He liked that description of hanging in bed with his man. Zander shuffled things around on his desk, as if looking for something, and only giving Justice part of his attention. "Yes, Whiskey stopped by. He said he had some questions for you."

Zander's blue gaze landed on Justice. "Pytor assures me you have him under control."

"He is mine."

For a moment, Zander eyed him, as if assessing the situation for himself. Finally, he gave Justice a sharp nod. "That's an interesting choice, but one I can respect. What were his questions?"

Justice shrugged. "He wouldn't share them with me."

"That doesn't sound like you have him under control."

Justice's gaze didn't waver. The last thing he wanted was for Zander to regret bringing him here. He couldn't go back to his old life. "You have nothing to worry about. The police love kicking up dust, hoping to trick us into giving up evidence that doesn't exist. Whiskey doesn't ask questions. I don't offer details. Our time together is spent doing other things."

A soft chuckle fell from Zander's lips. Humor flashed in his eyes. "Best of luck to you, then. We could use another good man on our side."

Justice dipped his chin but didn't respond. Whiskey would never be on their side. The man probably bled blue. He believed in the law. Like Zander, Justice believed in... justice. The two things were not synonymous. More times than not, no one kept the voiceless safe. There were real monsters around every corner. Neither Zander nor Justice could stomach that. Someone had to balance the scales.

"Oh, side note," Zander said, moving on. "I'm closing in on something in Vegas. In the next few days, I'll probably need you to head that way to take care of things. Take Pytor and Yaro. You'll need them on this one."

Justice nodded. "I'll be ready."

Pytor knocked once and entered without permission. He cast a quick look their way. "Sorry for the intrusion, boss. You have to see this." He grabbed the remote from the leather couch and powered on the TV. Justice turned toward the screen in the corner. It was a live news report. Blue and red lights flashed behind the blonde woman holding a microphone. She spoke fast. It took Justice a moment to follow, having caught things mid-speech.

"We're about five minutes away from Chief Baker releasing a formal statement on today's active shooter situation. But, right now, we know there are at least two confirmed dead with several more injured, including one police officer. The officer has been identified as Detective Whiskey Harris."

Whiskey's image appeared on the screen.

Justice flew to his feet. An inky black rage coated his brain. Someone had shot Whiskey.

"Detective Harris was rushed to Oceanside Medical. His condition is unknown at this time."

In an instant, Justice was headed for the door without looking back. Zander called his name, but Justice didn't slow. He had to find Whiskey. He had his phone to his ear before he made it to the car. Each time he tried Whiskey's cell, it went straight to voicemail. Justice fought the urge to scream like a maniac in a message.

"Call me right now," Justice growled instead.

He cursed and begged the universe as he drove across town. His mind raced. The news had said

Oceanside Medical. Unreal heavy traffic slowed him. Justice rocked in his seat, trying his best not to snap. Surely there was someone he could call. Hanging on to his sanity was always a challenge. This was hell. By the time he cleared the main entrance of the hospital, sweat coated his skin from the stress alone.

Justice spotted Easton waiting for an elevator to arrive. "Easton."

The tiny blond was all smiles when he turned Justice's way. Justice took it as a good sign. "Hey, you." His gaze moved over Justice. "Are you okay?"

Justice didn't bother answering or with pleasantries. "Have you seen Whiskey? What room is he in? I tried calling ahead, but they wouldn't tell me anything because of privacy laws."

Easton's face fell. "Whiskey is here? I didn't know. I come here a few days a week to visit some of the nurses."

Justice nodded. "I don't know who to contact to find out anything."

Easton grabbed his arm. "I've got this." He dragged Justice to the nurses' station. There wasn't a single face that didn't light up at the sight of him. Everyone took turns hugging Easton while Justice swallowed his silent screams. "I have a problem," Easton said, lowering his voice and drawing all the ladies in. "My friend is here, and I planned to visit, but I forget which room he's in. I tried calling him, but he's not answering. I don't know where to go."

A blonde nurse waved off his words. "That's no problem. What's his name?"

"Whiskey Harris."

She moved to the nearest computer and typed in the name. "He's still down in the ER. Room one thirty-two."

Justice was gone before he had time to thank anyone. He would make it up to Easton later. Knowing the room number got him easily buzzed through the locked ER door. Unfortunately, there was a cop posted outside Whiskey's door, no doubt stopping reporters who were much better at finding out info than Justice obviously was. They were stacked three deep, trying to get questions answered. Another set of cops was taking turns escorting them out.

Justice didn't waste any time lying his ass off. "I'm family."

The dark-haired cop eyed him but shook his head. "Sorry. No one goes in."

"Oh, I'm going in." He was ready to fight and go to jail. The door opened. A nurse slipped out and Justice caught sight of Whiskey. He slipped through the door while the nurse stood between him and the guard. The cop yelled behind him, but it was too late. He was at Whiskey's side and Whiskey was waving off the guard.

"Hey, baby," Whiskey rasped as Justice leaned over the edge of the bed and went to work trying to see Whiskey's injuries for himself.

"I tried to call, but you didn't answer. Then no one would tell me your room number. Easton got the info for me, but then this guy wouldn't let me in. Jesus Christ. What happened? What does the doctor say?"

Whiskey stroked his arms, openly trying to soothe him. "It's okay. Calm down."

Justice took a breath and finally focused on Whiskey's face. He was alive and obviously stable. Justice took another breath. Fuck it. Air wasn't enough. He leaned in and pressed his lips to Whiskey's. He didn't move away or deepen their kiss. Justice needed the contact of skin on skin. He needed to feel Whiskey's breath and know he still lived. This was awful. It would kill him if anything happened to Whiskey.

"I'll wait outside."

Until the words were spoken, Justice didn't

realize they weren't alone. A large bald guy slipped out without looking back.

"That's Leo. Another detective on the force." Whiskey still sounded like there was something wrong with his voice. "I don't know where my cellphone is, or I would've called. Everything happened so fast. How did you know I was here?"

"It was on the news." Justice still didn't move away. He couldn't.

"Fuck," Whiskey rasped. "That means my parents probably heard the same way. There's no phone in here."

"You haven't told me what happened." Justice didn't give a fuck about anyone else. He needed to know everything.

Whiskey blinked. He looked high as hell. "Yeah. Sorry." He blinked again. "Some guy shot up the mall."

Justice blew out an aggravated breath. A snort escaped him. Whiskey was awake and talking. There weren't any nurses or doctors fighting to help Whiskey. He would be okay. Still, Justice wanted to know everything. "I know that much, baby. I meant you. How bad are your injuries?"

"Oh. Sorry. Flesh wounds." He pushed down the sheet covering him and lifted his hospital gown.

Whiskey was nude beneath. It seemed they had stolen his clothes. His midriff was completely covered in bandages. "One bullet caught me in the side." He dropped the gown and motioned toward his neck and a smaller bandage. "Another grazed me here. Got lucky as hell," he said, sounding ready to pass out.

Justice's eyes fell closed. Now that he knew Whiskey would be okay, the shock had his insides shaking. Before Whiskey, Justice never felt anything. Now he felt everything, and it was fucking awful. His eyes opened. Whiskey still held his arm, but his eyes were closed. His chest rose and fell with every breath he took. Justice watched it happen. Nothing else mattered at the moment. When he had Whiskey home, and he had a moment to breathe, he would make sure the bastard who had shot his man was dead. Then maybe he would be able to breathe again.

JUSTICE COULDN'T STOP HOVERING. HE GOT THE impression, by the number of huffs Whiskey suppressed, he was getting a little tired of being babied.

"You know, I can still walk," Whiskey said, after the third time of Justice refusing to let him get dressed.

Justice set one knee on the bed and leaned in, kissing Whiskey's leg. "I know you can." He moved higher and kissed Whiskey's knee. "But I think you should stay right where you are." He skimmed his lips up Whiskey's thigh. "And cuddle with me," he finished as he settled in and gently scooped Whiskey into his arms. His lips found the spot below Whiskey's ear. "You should humor me, sexy. I haven't gotten over thinking I might lose you."

"One more day." Whiskey sounded lovingly exasperated. "I have to go back to work tomorrow."

That wasn't exactly true. Justice just hadn't found a way to broach the topic with Whiskey yet. He decided this was possibly the best opening he would get. "About that, you know you don't have to work, right? I make enough to support you."

A bright smile lit Whiskey's face. "While I do what? I'm not the type to sit around all day."

"Something less dangerous." Even Justice heard the childish grumble in his tone.

For a moment, Whiskey's gaze moved over Justice's face, as if searching for something. "I love you," he said finally.

"I love you too."

Whiskey gave him a sharp nod. "Then please don't try to change me. I worked hard for this job and I'm good at it. There's nothing I can say that'll make you worry less, but I won't ever willingly leave you. You can depend on that."

Justice didn't feel better, but he also didn't know how to fight. Loving someone was new for him. He settled onto his side with his arm pillowing his head. For a minute, he simply stared at Whiskey. Whiskey had no clue how unique he was to Justice. If he knew Justice at all, he would be terrified. Most would consider Justice a sociopath at best. He didn't date or fall in love. Life had beaten all emotion from him more years ago than he could recall. Justice imagined someone must have gotten under his skin when he was younger, but he couldn't remember anyone. He didn't consider himself gay or straight. Justice was nothing. He was an empty shell. Then, Whiskey had looked at Justice like he saw a soul where there wasn't one. Something had fired to life inside Justice. He didn't know how to stamp it out now.

Justice could tell by Whiskey's expression he wouldn't be moved. "Your mom called," Justice said, letting things go for now.

Whiskey chuckled. "Is it weird that she only calls you now?"

Justice kissed Whiskey's shoulder. "No. Not at all. She's worried about disturbing you while you're resting." He knew that wasn't what Whiskey meant. Since Justice had called her from the hospital, reassuring Whiskey's mother that Whiskey was fine, she hadn't stopped calling Justice. Once she had shown up and realized exactly who Justice was to Whiskey, and that they were now living together, there had been no stopping her. It seemed Shelby had been waiting forever for her son to finally introduce her to someone. She didn't care at all about Justice being a man. Shelby just wanted to be a bigger part of her son's life.

"Everyone is acting like I'm on the edge of death. I'm fine. Sore, but fine."

"You're sore? What can I do? Do you need a pain pill?"

Whiskey pinched the spot between his eyes. He drew a slow, audible breath. "Okay," he said, rolling to his knees and straddling Justice's hips before Justice could stop him.

"Baby, no. You'll tear open your stitches."

"Hush."

Justice blinked. Whiskey was never short or disobedient.

"Don't worry. I won't do anything to hurt myself," Whiskey promised. He sat back on his heels. "Look, baby. I get it. If anything happened to you, I would not be okay. But I need you to trust that I want to come home to you too badly to let anything happen to me. Plus," he said, bracing his weight on his hands and lowering his head until he was inches from Justice's lips. "I have no intention of missing this." He skimmed his lips across Justice's mouth. Whiskey moved lower, brushing light kisses down Justice's neck before moving to his collarbone.

Justice buried his fingers in Whiskey's hair. He didn't want Whiskey to stop, but Justice also couldn't shake the fear he had felt over learning Whiskey had been shot. Justice needed Whiskey to be well. "Please don't hurt yourself."

Whiskey's hands found their way beneath Justice's shirt. "Don't make me get my handcuffs. I will chain you to this bed. Let me have what I want."

Goddamn it. He would give Whiskey anything. Justice tilted his head back and sucked air as Whiskey shoved his shirt higher and moved lower. Whiskey shuffled down the bed and circled Justice's navel with his tongue. Justice's eyes fell closed. He scratched at the covers for purchase as Whiskey peeled Justice's pajama pants down one hip and kissed Justice's hipbone.

"I love you so much," Whiskey said against Justice's skin so quietly Justice swore he felt the words more than heard them.

"Goddamn." The breathless curse escaped Justice with no input from his brain. Reaching above him, Justice grabbed the headboard and held on. Whiskey tugged Justice's pants lower until Justice's erection sprang free. He licked Justice's shaft from root to tip. Justice's hips left the bed, chasing Whiskey's tongue.

"You're so goddamn gorgeous." Whiskey swallowed Justice's cock before Justice could rub two thoughts together. Whiskey had enthusiasm. Justice was so in love and turned on that his brain wouldn't work.

"Let's both quit our jobs and do this all day."

Whiskey chuckled around Justice's erection. The sound vibrated through Justice's shaft, making Justice gasp. He was already on edge and ready to blow. Right when Justice tensed, an orgasm within reach, Whiskey stopped. Justice gasped for air and writhed. Whiskey shot upward and claimed Justice's mouth. As their tongues met, Whiskey rocked against Justice, sending him flying. Justice clung to Whiskey, shaking and kissing him deep while cum coated his man's clothes. He hadn't done a single damn thing in his life to deserve Whiskey. That didn't mean he would ever let Whiskey go. One way or another, he would find a way to keep Whiskey safe. No one would ever touch his man again.

SIX

DESK DUTY SUCKED ASS. Whiskey had never liked paperwork. Now, here he was, stuck on the world's oldest computer all day. The low res screen would blind him before long. He swore to himself he would bring donuts to the guys stuck doing this from now on. This was some bullshit. He couldn't understand how anyone kept their sanity with this slow of internet. Whiskey had never been closer to quitting.

Leo's bald head popped over the top of the massive machine built by the devil. His amber eyes flashed with concern. "How are you feeling?"

Whiskey tried smoothing out his scowl without luck. "Like someone shot me and I'm being punished for it with dial-up."

A bright smile lit Leo's face. "You're not being punished. It's desk duty. Nice. Easy. Safe. Desk duty." Whiskey scratched his nose with his middle finger. A deep rumble of laughter escaped the giant cop. His face cleared. Leo looked serious again. Also, slightly uncomfortable. "I have to say, I was really surprised to learn who you're dating. No one here saw that one coming."

Whiskey fought a blush. He cleared his throat. "Yeah. Um." Damn. He hadn't exactly expected to come out at work. Justice busting into his hospital room hadn't left him much of a choice. "I guess I don't really talk about my private life. Not many people know I'm gay."

Leo's eyebrows snapped together in a frown. "Don't nobody give a fuck about that. I'm talking about who you're dating. The last thing I expected was to see one of Kapra's men busting into your room."

Irritation owned Whiskey. "Justice is an accountant. I'd hardly consider him one of Kapra's men."

Leo held up his hands, showing his surrender. "All right. Don't shoot the messenger. I just thought you might want a heads up that it doesn't look good. I imagine it won't go over well with the powers that be."

Whiskey's scowl didn't budge, even after Leo wandered away. If someone he considered a friend was this upset about Justice, Whiskey couldn't imagine what his boss would think. His gaze moved back to the ancient computer. Did Leo know something he didn't? Damn. Why didn't he ever ask questions? The moment he had learned Justice worked for Zander Kapra, he should have demanded answers. He definitely should have recognized the danger to his job. The thing was, at first, he had just been so damn wowed by Justice. By the time any red flags waved, it was too late. He was in love with Justice. Whiskey believed in him. He couldn't imagine Justice doing anything illegal. Justice was just so damn amazing. Whiskey didn't want to consider the possibility of Justice doing anything outside the law.

Whiskey bit his lip. Fuck it. Whiskey needed to know if he had something to worry about. He typed Justice's name into the database. It took the million-year-old device forever to run the name. Whiskey chewed the side of his nail and bobbed his foot. If Justice came back with a file, Whiskey had no idea what he would do about it. He didn't want to lose Justice. The computer dinged. No results found. Unfortunately, Whiskey didn't feel better. Maybe if Justice had a parking violation or something, Whiskey could have laughed off the hollow feeling in his gut that Leo's words caused. Instead, his dread deepened. He switched search parameters and hit enter again. There was nothing. He changed them again. Nothing.

Whiskey stared at the screen. He couldn't breathe. There was no record of a Justice Alexander anywhere. No police record, driver's license, or property listed to that name. Justice didn't exist. He ran Justice's address. Whiskey wondered if he would be sick while he waited. It came back listed under Zander Kapra. Whiskey's eyes fell closed.

"Harris!"

Whiskey jumped at the sound of his name yelled across the office. He glanced up to find his boss, red-faced and waiting. His gaze automatically slid Leo's way.

"Told you so," Leo mouthed, making Whiskey's heart sink. He pushed to his feet, wincing more against the situation than the pain. Justice was completely amazing. It didn't make sense for this to be happening to his life. Whiskey just hoped he wasn't about to lose everything. He wasn't mentally prepared for that to happen today. Whiskey still hadn't wrapped his mind around Justice not existing. Fuck. He didn't know what to think.

JUSTICE PACED THE FLOOR AND WATCHED THE clock. Two more hours and Whiskey would be home. Damn. He didn't know when he had turned into this needy mess. Justice wanted to get in his car, drive down to Whiskey's work, and steal him away. They could go anywhere. Travel the world. He didn't want to lie anymore.

"When are you coming back to work?"

Justice turned the question over in his mind. He owed everything to Zander Kapra. "Where's Yaro and Pytor?" Justice asked instead of answering.

Zander smiled and shook his head. He was such a gorgeous guy. It didn't surprise Justice at all that he had caught the Conti's eye all those years ago. That one horrible act led to all this. Everything Justice owned was thanks to Zander's pain. How did he repay that and hang on to Whiskey? Justice was at a loss.

"I wouldn't abandon you."

Zander's blue gaze latched on to Justice and didn't move. A kind smile touched his lips. "You're free here, Justice. You don't owe me anything. If anyone understands falling in love with someone good, it's me."

Justice's throat swelled. "I owe you everything." Zander understood like most never would. He knew what it was like to starve and kill. To find himself pitted against his best friend and be forced to choose. He knew what it was like to watch his brother die at the hands of a monster.

"Tell us how we can help," Adrik said, chiming in.

Justice glanced Adrik's way. Adrik pushed his glasses up his nose. He looked so much like an innocent and slightly nerdy teen. Looks were deceiving. "No one can help me with this, but thank you. I'm coming back to work. It's just that today was Whiskey's first day back since the shooting. I'm worried he won't hold up well and need me when he gets home. If he does okay, I'll be back tomorrow. I'm not saying I'll be sane, but I'll be there. Fuck. I don't know how people do this normal shit, worrying all the time."

Zander snorted. "You trust that you fell in love

with a strong, brave man who can take care of himself. Don't forget, he walked away from getting shot. The guy who shot him didn't."

Justice nodded. He knew. "He's amazing." He motioned impatiently, moving on. "Let's get to work so you two can get on with your day."

Adrik and Zander both stared at him in silence.

"What?"

Adrik pushed his glasses up his nose again. They did nothing to hide his eerie light eyes. He fiddled with the laptop in his lap. Adrik cleared his throat. "Have you thought about telling your man what you do? We could use a few more cops on the payroll. I know you don't think he'll understand, but I'm not so sure."

They both stared at him expectantly. Justice thought he might hyperventilate. They didn't know Whiskey. He would not forgive Justice. "This isn't up for discussion."

Adrik dropped his gaze to his laptop, as if he couldn't handle Justice's gruff tone. He immediately felt like shit. Before he could apologize, Zander chimed in. "You've changed. He's changed you. For the better, of course, but— eventually—you'll have to be honest with him. Trust me, he will not take being lied to kindly. If you want to be with this guy forever, you'll need a middle ground."

Justice pinched the spot between his eyes where pain bloomed. He knew Zander was right, but he needed more time. Justice hadn't figured out yet how to keep Whiskey and his job. Both were equally important to his humanity.

"Maybe if he met me," Adrik suggested. "I don't mind telling him my story, if you think it would win him to our side."

Justice counted to ten inside his head so he wouldn't scare Adrik again. "No one could listen to you and be unmoved, sweetie. I'll think about it. Okay?"

Adrik's face lit—like Justice heaped praise on him.

Zander gave him a barely susceptible nod, letting Justice know he had chosen the right words. "Let's get this show on the road and get out of here before Justice's man comes home."

Justice breathed a sigh of relief. The topic was dead for now. He knew he couldn't avoid talking to Whiskey forever. Eventually, he would have to find a way to explain all this. God, he hoped he could find a way to keep Whiskey. Otherwise, heaven help the world if he lost him.

FOR LONGER THAN WHISKEY CARED TO ADMIT, he stared at the front door of the home he shared with Justice with no plan. His heart ached. He was honest enough to admit he had fallen hard for Justice. Whiskey didn't know how to lose him. Then again, Whiskey had never had Justice. Not really. With nothing left for it, Whiskey knocked.

Justice's eyes flashed with heat as he opened the door. Even his smile was hungry. It lasted only as long as it took for Justice to register Whiskey's expression. "Why are you knocking? You live here. What's wrong?"

"I got suspended today."

"For getting shot?" Justice sounded outraged as he stepped aside and hauled Whiskey inside.

Standing inside the foyer with nothing but his shattered heart, Whiskey eyed Justice, wondering if Justice truly believed Whiskey was dumb. Maybe he was stupid as hell. God knew he felt like it. "No. For dating you."

Justice's expression snapped closed.

Whiskey waited, praying Justice would say something. Anything. Silence dragged on. Whiskey broke. "Wow. You've got nothing, huh? Maybe you could start by telling me your real name?"

Justice's chest expanded on a deep breath. "It's Justice Alexandrov."

The air left Whiskey's lungs on a whoosh. He nodded. A name was something. It was a place to start. "What do you really do for Zander Kapra?"

Justice's expression never showed a hint of emotion. "You don't want to know that."

Whiskey's eyes fell closed. It hurt worse than he ever imagined. If Justice had punched him in the chest and ripped out his heart, it would have hurt less. He forced his eyes open. Whiskey needed to know. "Did you set out to seduce me because of what I do? To throw me off some trail?"

A muscle in Justice's jaw flexed.

For a full minute, Whiskey wondered if the pain would kill him. Surely no one could live after suffering this much at the hands of someone they loved. He fought the urge to tell Justice exactly how much damage he had done. Whiskey wanted to scream and break shit. His throat hurt too badly. "I wish I could go back to the night we met and tell myself to walk right past you." Even to Whiskey's ears, his voice sounded ragged.

Justice crowded his space, looking enraged. His nostrils flared and his eyes flashed with open anger. "You didn't walk right by me, did you? The minute you met my stare, it was too late. You are mine. There's no going back."

An unexpected burst of humor flashed through Whiskey. There wasn't a goddamn thing funny about any of this, but Whiskey still fought the urge to laugh. He was done. In fact, he would venture to say he had never been more done in his whole goddamn life. "No."

Justice's eyebrows rose. "No?"

Whiskey set his palms on Justice's hard chest. His heart skipped a beat, and he wanted to cry as the warmth of Justice's hard chest seeped into his palms. Justice's heart beat beneath his hand. He loved this man. Rather, he loved who he thought Justice was. Whiskey nodded. "That's what I said. No. It's not too late for me. You see, I'm unfucking myself." He pushed, forcing Justice to step back. "Loving you hurts. It's fake. A lie. So I'm taking back my heart. I'm untangling myself from your web of deceit. Whatever happens, happens. If you decide to kill me or I land in prison because of you, then just know that I'll be taking my heart with me wherever I go. You have no place with me anymore."

Something crossed Justice's features before his usual mask fell back into place. It looked a lot like hurt. "You don't get to make me love you, tell me you love me too, and then walk away."

"I don't love you." The words felt like a thousand tiny knives in Whiskey's heart. "I love who I thought you were. That man isn't real. My Justice doesn't exist." Whiskey swallowed past the pain of admitting that aloud. "You're a stranger to me."

The pain Whiskey thought he had spotted only moments earlier made an appearance and didn't budge. Justice stared at him with all the hurt, anger, and longing Whiskey felt. When he responded, his voice shook with emotion. Justice was realer than he had ever seen him. "You know me. No one else has seen as much of the real me as you have, but I don't know how to make you believe."

Whiskey wanted to believe. God only knew how badly he wished Justice were a real person who had swept him off his feet. "You can't." Even Whiskey heard the pain in that harsh whisper. "You're a thousand lies too deep for me to trust you again." Pain sideswiped Whiskey as the truth settled in—he had lost everything. "I'm sure destroying me means nothing to you. After all, that was the point, right? Seduce me and keep me looking the other way."

"No. I—"

Whiskey stepped around Justice and headed for the door, refusing to listen to whatever lie Justice told next. As he opened the door, Justice slammed into him. His arm shot over Whiskey's shoulder and smacked the door closed. He kept his palm pressed against the door, holding it closed. His lips skimmed Whiskey's ear. "We're not finished here."

Whiskey fought for air. He had never felt so much anguish that it made it hard to inflate his lungs. Whiskey was there now. "Don't worry," Whiskey said, hearing the growl in his voice and incapable of stopping. "I'm not coming after you. You got your way. I lost everything." Whiskey pressed his forehead to the door, praying his knees wouldn't give out. "You should've killed me. It would've hurt less." Whiskey yanked, tearing the door open despite Justice's attempts at keeping it held closed. It seemed Whiskey's rage was stronger than Justice's anger.

"Goddam it, Whiskey," Justice roared. His words were heavily accented, making Whiskey wonder how he had kept it hidden all this time. "I fucking love you. That's not a lie."

Whiskey's knees buckled, but he managed to stay upright by sheer will. All he had was his pride.

He would be taking that with him too. Whiskey didn't look back as he walked away. He had swallowed enough lies in the past six months to last a lifetime. Whiskey couldn't handle another damn thing.

SEVEN

THE SMELL OF COFFEE, cake, and books mixed together to smack Whiskey in the face and weaken his knees. He had to admit the combination of a bookstore and bakery had been a great idea. The place catered to people like him—a book and sweets lover. Easton glanced up from the cupcakes he was decorating. A huge smile lit his face. He dropped his icing bag and circled the counter.

"Detective Harris. Did you actually come to see me?"

Whiskey accepted his hug. Easton was so tiny and fragile. He was a sprite. It was odd knowing he was married to Nicolaus. Nico was the opposite of Easton in every way. They shouldn't fit. Yet they did.

"Please, call me Whiskey. I thought we had gotten past this."

Easton's green eyes sparkled. "Meh. Would you like some coffee?"

"I would love that. Thank you." Whiskey's heart warmed. He didn't really have friends. Whiskey had never made time for them. Before now, Whiskey hadn't felt the loss. He didn't know why he had sought out Easton. Maybe he needed to be close to someone who had already survived the worst. Maybe then Whiskey would feel like he might live through this.

Easton poured him a cup while talking over his shoulder. "Where's that sexy guy you had with you at the wedding?"

Whiskey took a slow breath. It didn't help. He cleared his throat. "Turns out, he's not who he claimed to be, so I guess that's over."

Easton eyed him for a moment, as if assessing the situation. Finally, he motioned toward a small two-person table in the corner. "Take this over there. I'll be there in a second," Easton said, handing over the coffee.

Whiskey dutifully carried his drink to the table. He doctored it while he waited. His gaze scanned the room. A familiar figure caught his eye. Justice lounged in the opposite corner. He was inside the bookstore side of the building and held a book, but his blue gaze was locked on Whiskey. Whiskey's heartbeat pounded in his ears. Justice didn't look away. Easton joined Whiskey, bringing along his own cup of coffee, and pulling Whiskey's gaze away from Justice.

He settled in across from Whiskey. "Okay. Tell me how he's not who he claimed to be."

Was Justice following him? This couldn't be a coincidence. Could it? Whiskey cleared his throat and tried to think. "He's pretty literally not who he said he was," Whiskey admitted, feeling defeated. His gaze dropped to his coffee. A humorless smile touched Whiskey's lips as the full impact of losing Justice hit him all over again. "I bought a ring."

"Oh, sweetie," Easton said, sounding hurt on Whiskey's behalf. "That's heartbreaking. Are things really unsalvageable with...?" Easton flashed him a pain smiled. "Sorry. I don't recall his name."

Whiskey fought the urge to look Justice's way. "It's Justice."

A bright smile lit Easton's entire face. "Oh, wow. How fitting. It's like he was made for you."

The ache in Whiskey's chest grew. He massaged

the spot that tightened by the second. "He works for Zander Kapra."

Easton blinked. "I don't know who that is."

"He owns Luna Hotel and Casino. All of them on the West Coast, actually."

"Okay." Easton dragged out the word. "Do you have a problem with gambling? I'm confused."

Whiskey shifted uncomfortably. He felt a bit like he was corrupting someone's innocence. "Mafia, sweetie. All betting and prize fights are controlled by the mafia."

Easton's expression never changed. "Oh. So."

"I'm a cop."

"So."

Whiskey had a hard time understanding why Easton was unmoved. "I got suspended and all my old cases are under review now pending further investigation, just by association."

"Well." Easton straightened his spine. "He definitely shouldn't have lied," Easton said, obviously trying to be on Whiskey's side. "That's never good."

An unexpected laugh bubbled in Whiskey's throat. "Why do I get the feeling there's a but coming?"

Easton flashed him a guilty-looking smile. One of

his shoulders lifted in a half shrug. "Well, I mean, it's just a job, isn't it?"

"Which one? His or mine?"

"Both," Easton said without missing a beat. "If you love him and he loves you, why can't one of you give? Do you both have jobs you love so much that you would lose each other to keep them? If so, you're definitely better off finding someone else, because that's not love." Easton covered Whiskey's hand with his. Whiskey immediately dropped his gaze to the table at the contact. Tiny white scars covered Easton's knuckles. They were by no means the worst of Easton's scars, but they were the ones that showed how hard he had fought for his life. It hit Whiskey. Justice's knuckles were the same. He didn't have the hands of an accountant. Justice had the hands of a survivor. "I'm sorry, sweetie," Easton said, pulling his attention back on topic. "I'll always be one hundred percent on your side. No matter what. But even though this place is my pride and joy and it saved me when I didn't want to go on, I would dump this bakery in a heartbeat for Nico. Nothing means more than him. That's love." Easton pulled away and Whiskey found himself holding Easton's gaze. "Don't settle for anything less than someone you would give everything to keep."

Against his will, Whiskey's gaze slid back Justice's way. He was gone. The pain was almost unbearable. Maybe he needed to be honest with himself. Could he live without his job? Was it more important than Justice? Fuck, though. Justice had still lied. He had still set out to seduce Whiskey for nefarious reasons... right? Goddamn it. He didn't know anything anymore. Suddenly, Whiskey needed to say the words that pounded at his brain. He couldn't take another second of staying silent on the one thing that drove him to near insanity. Easton was the only person there to listen. Whiskey broke. "He must be the greatest actor on the planet, because—when he said he loved me—I believed it. Like to my soul, I believed him."

Easton pressed his lips together, looking pained —like he tried to hold back his words. He didn't make it. "Oh, babe. Maybe he did mean it. You have to fight. I saw him the day you were shot. He was in a panic at the idea of anything happening to you. You'll never forgive yourself if you only save yourself."

Fuck if that wasn't exactly what Whiskey was doing—saving himself. Justice had looked desperate when Whiskey walked away. He had looked like he wouldn't survive without Whiskey, but Whiskey had run. Could he live with knowing he hadn't asked every question and learned every answer? Could he live without fighting? He wasn't a goddamn quitter. The unanswered questions would kill him. But things had to be on his terms. Whiskey couldn't let Justice be in charge this time. Whiskey was too weak when it came to Justice. But he had to know everything before he could move on. They wouldn't be over until Whiskey knew if every minute had been a lie. They wouldn't be finished until Whiskey knew if Justice's love was an act.

THE NIGHTS WERE THE WORST. REALISTICALLY, Justice understood he had lived his entire life without Whiskey before six months ago. That didn't matter to Justice's heart. He couldn't stop doing the things they had done together, torturing himself with Whiskey's absence. As he stared at the ocean from the lounge chair he always shared with Whiskey, Justice questioned if he could go on. If Whiskey never forgave him or came home, Justice was scared of his reaction. He might do anything. Truth be told, he had never really been all that mentally stable. He couldn't do his job if sanity ever came into play. So, without Whiskey, Justice couldn't say if he would decide to keep going. Fifty-one years was a long life of bullshit. Maybe he didn't have another year left in him.

Nighttime always had him at his weakest. Justice just wanted to be with Whiskey. He no longer knew how. He could quit his job and confess his sins, but none of that wiped away the lies. Things looked hopeless.

"What a fucked-up bunch we all turned out to be," Nico said, appearing from the shadows. He filled the chair to Justice's left and set his helmet on his knee.

Justice took a swig from the bottle of vodka resting on his stomach. He wished he had the ability to get drunk. Alcohol did nothing for him any longer. That was the Russian in him. "You always were a sneaky fuck for such a big bastard."

A soft chuckle rumbled through the air. "I was not quiet. You are getting old."

"I've been old for a long time now. Tired," he added, taking another drink.

"Tell me how to help," Nico said quietly, sounding like the true friend he had always been. "I owe you much."

Bitterness welled inside Justice. Not toward

Nico, but at life. He didn't know anyone who hadn't suffered the worst of everything. He didn't understand how such an ugly world could keep turning daily with even semi-functioning people left onboard. All life did was pour constant bullshit on everyone, daring them to keep going with nothing left. It was wrong. "You owe me nothing. Those boys who hurt Easton got what they deserved. All I did was ensure they're never found. People like your pretty Easton deserve to cling to the light only they see. The rest of us are too fucked to be saved. We may as well take a few of the worst with us to hell."

For a long while, Nico sat with him in silence. When he finally spoke, he sounded hesitant. "When I saw you at the wedding, you looked different. Happy. I thought... I hoped you would find with Whiskey what I've found with Easton. Whiskey seemed an odd choice, but we don't get to choose. Not really."

A ridiculous realization hit Justice. He wanted to talk about Whiskey. In any capacity. Justice needed to feel like Whiskey wasn't so far away. "What do you mean Whiskey is an odd choice? He is perfect."

It helped that Nico didn't look at him. He kept staring at the horizon while keeping up his end of things. "He isn't sweet—like Easton, I suppose. I guess, like me, I assumed you would like a soft place after all the years of hardship. Whiskey is a lot like us. He does not have the rainbow-colored view of life to offset you."

A smile tugged at the corners of Justice's mouth. It was true. Whiskey would never be soft and malleable. "I am much too dark for a rainbow. If Whiskey was like your Easton, I would crush him." A new ache slashed through him. "I suppose I still destroyed him, nonetheless." He polished off the bottle and set it aside. "It's also very likely a person cannot take as much life as I have and expect the universe's mercy. I certainly can't expect Whiskey's forgiveness."

Nico turned his head. His gaze locked on to Justice. "Are you sorry? I'm not," he added before looking away again.

That was a fair point. He stared at the ocean, wishing like hell he could hold Whiskey. His fingers curled into a fist, trying to cope with the loss of holding him. He had cut his heart out long ago because he couldn't face who he was. Then, Whiskey had somehow grown the organ back. Now Justice was stuck staring at the pain of who he was and used to be. It was all so damn ugly. He couldn't blame Whiskey for wanting no part of it.

"I used to think I had no choice," Justice said, admitting something he never had. "Gio brought me here and set me in front of those other boys. It was kill or be killed. Just the same as going to war, right?" Nico didn't answer, obviously seeing his statement for the rhetorical question it was. Justice turned inside himself, wishing he didn't still see their faces. Gio Conti had been an evil bastard, shipping kids into the country for his underground fights. They were brutal and heavily bet upon. Justice hadn't been given a choice. At the time, he hadn't seen another option than to do as told. Now he recognized he had always had a choice. He could have chosen to be the one who died. Maybe he should have. The person who left that life wasn't a person anymore. Not really. No matter how much polish Zander applied, trying to atone for Gio's brutality. "There were no winners," Justice said more to himself. He would never be able to share himself with Whiskey, and he knew that was what it would take to get him back. Some stories could not be told. They locked the tongue and froze the brain. There were no words in any language to describe hell. Yeah, he probably wouldn't make it much longer without Whiskey.

THE RESTAURANT WAS DEAD FOR LUNCHTIME. Still, Whiskey noticed Justice chose a table on the opposite side of the room. He stayed within eyesight but out of earshot. Whiskey couldn't look away from him. As usual, he was dressed nice, but he looked a little ragged around the edges. He needed a shave. The top two buttons of his shirt were undone, showing a hint of the tattoo he usually kept hidden beneath. There were dark circles beneath his eyes. Whiskey didn't want to care about any of that, but he did. Love didn't disappear because he didn't want it. Unfortunately, life didn't work that way.

Leo slid into the booth across from him. He glanced over his shoulder, following Whiskey's gaze before focusing on Whiskey. "Which of you is stalking the other?"

Whiskey met the man's amber stare. "I'm not sure anymore."

With a shake of his head, Leo slid the upside-down coffee cup on a saucer to the edge of the table and flipped it right side up. A red-haired waitress moved to fill it. Whiskey flipped his over too, letting her fill his cup as well.

They both nodded their thanks before Whiskey focused on Leo again. "What made you want to meet?"

One of Leo's giant shoulders lifted in a half shrug as he doctored his coffee. "I just wanted to check on you. Also, I wanted to let you know that I backed up your story. I told Mike you hadn't known about Justice's ties to Kapra and you'd ended things when you found out."

Whiskey listened without a hint of care. He had been a good cop. If his work didn't speak for itself, then fuck it. "You didn't have to do that."

"I did," Leo said, holding his stare. "You're one of the good ones. Everyone knows it." A small smile touched Leo's lips. "Hell, if I'd known there was even a small chance you would've accepted, I would've thrown my hat in the ring for your attention. I always thought you were straight."

It took every ounce of Whiskey's concentration to hide his shock. "Same."

A soft and surprisingly sexy chuckle rumbled from Leo. "I guess neither of us really knows each other."

Whiskey shook his head, fighting a smile. "I guess not." Leo was big and handsome, but Whiskey had nothing left to give anyone.

Leo laughed. His smile grew. "In a way, I guess I did get you out on a date. You're here."

Whiskey snorted before a loud sigh escaped him. "If my life wasn't such a mess, I'd agree."

Laughter still flashed in Leo's eyes. "Hey, say what you want. I'm still going to tell people this was a date. They'll be jealous."

Despite Leo's outrageous words, Whiskey was grateful for his company. He was weaker today than ever. He wasn't sure he would make it through the rest of the day beneath Justice's heated stare. Whiskey had no idea what the hell he was supposed to do. All he knew was, he loved and missed Justice. He was hopeless. Luckily, he hadn't had time to let his duplex go before everything fell apart, but more than half his stuff was still at Justice's. Whiskey hadn't wanted to be alone with him to figure out how to get it back. He was starting to think it would cost him less to buy all new things. Being alone with Justice might cost his soul.

"Oh, by the way, we made an arrest in that body in the freezer case."

He had Whiskey's attention. "Really?"

Leo nodded while staring at the menu. "Turns out, it was some guy he was trading kiddie porn with. The guy thought he would get caught up in the freezer guy's latest molestation trial. So he killed him before he could talk."

Whiskey shrugged. "Well, two more sickos off the street, I suppose. Sounds like a good day to me."

"Yep," Leo said, sounding distracted.

Whiskey's gaze slid Justice's way again. For a moment, they stared at each other without looking away. Whiskey's throat swelled. He wanted to go home, and he didn't mean to his tiny, empty duplex. That wasn't his home anymore. Whiskey wanted to be where his heart lived, and he didn't know if that would ever happen again. He had never felt lonelier.

THERE WAS A SMALL PART OF JUSTICE THAT wanted to rage over constantly watching Whiskey meet other men. First, it had been Easton and now Leo. The thing was, Whiskey's gaze always returned to Justice. Once Leo left, Whiskey looked Justice's way and hadn't turned away since. Neither of them blinked. Even with an entire room between them, their stare was a connection. Justice tried willing the distance between them away. Maybe Whiskey would never forgive him. Justice didn't care. Any penance, whatever Whiskey asked, Justice would willingly give as long as Whiskey didn't take away his love. He wouldn't stop. Every day from now until the end of time, Justice would follow on Whiskey's heels, stalking him to the ends of the earth. Maybe his love was sick and twisted. Unhealthy. Justice didn't have a fuck to give. He wasn't like other people. Justice didn't quit.

As Justice looked on, Whiskey came to his feet. Hope rose in Justice's chest. Whiskey didn't look happy. He didn't smile. There was no triumph in Justice. Only need. Justice tilted his chin up as Whiskey came to stand over him.

"Justice Alexandrov. You're under arrest for stalking."

For a moment, Justice could only blink. He couldn't find his voice. Finally, he managed a rasp through the pain. "Is that so?"

Whiskey made an impatient gesture for Justice to stand. "Let's go. Don't force me to make a scene."

Justice shrugged. Under arrest or not, at least he would get to spend a few minutes with Whiskey. He slid from the booth, got out his wallet, and dropped a few bills on the table. Whiskey eyed his every move.

"As a courtesy for our history together, I won't handcuff you until we're outside. Don't make me regret that decision."

Justice met his stare. "Kinky." There wasn't a hint of emotion in his voice. Justice imagined it said a lot of bad things about him that he didn't care what happened to him as long as he was with Whiskey. He willingly walked to Whiskey's vehicle. The moment they were standing beside Whiskey's truck, Justice obediently put his hands behind his back and waited. There was a small part of him that still believed Whiskey wasn't really arresting him. Then the handcuffs snapped around his wrist. Justice dropped his chin and stared at his feet. His throat ached. He recognized in that moment exactly how sick he was, because they were together and that was enough for him. Even once the handcuffs were locked in place, Whiskey didn't immediately move away. The tip of his finger stroked Justice's palm. His eyes burned. Before he could decide if the light touch had been real, Whiskey helped him into the passenger seat and shut him inside. Justice followed Whiskey with his gaze as he circled the front of the truck and climbed behind the wheel. He stared so hard at Whiskey's profile; he knew there was no way in hell that Whiskey didn't feel his gaze like a physical touch.

"You look gorgeous."

Whiskey didn't look his way. "You look a mess."

That was because he was a disaster without Whiskey. He had always hated himself. Now, that was all he felt twenty-four-seven. Without Whiskey's love, Justice had nothing holding him together. Without Whiskey's love, Justice was back to the emptiness of no emotions. It was no longer comfortable or quiet. It was cold.

"I don't sleep without you."

"Please just be quiet."

Justice locked his teeth at Whiskey's request. He couldn't give Whiskey anything else. Whiskey had taken away that right. The least Justice could do was give Whiskey what peace he could. God knew he had fucked up everything else.

As Whiskey pulled into Justice's driveway, he expected Justice would have something to say. He didn't react at all. He hadn't made a sound since Whiskey asked him to stop talking. Even as Whiskey walked Justice to the front door and let him inside, Justice didn't ask for his key back or question him.

At the edge of the bed, Whiskey released one of Justice's wrists and patted him down. He found a gun strapped his leg.

Whiskey pulled it out and held it up. "Really, Justice? For fuck's sake. Get on the bed."

Justice complied. Whiskey worked the cuffs through the rung of the headboard. He thought his nerves would snap before he had Justice's wrists cuffed to the headboard. It didn't matter Justice hadn't resisted or argued once. He had quietly accepted everything Whiskey did. Still, Whiskey wasn't sure he could keep his shit together much longer. He was so goddamn angry and hurt. All because he loved Justice. No amount of lies had destroyed even an ounce of Whiskey's feelings for Justice. They were supposed to be a team. Justice would fucking talk to him or he would stay cuffed to the bed until they both died from thirst.

Whiskey sat on the edge of the bed at Justice's hip and stared at the wall. He didn't know where to start or what he hoped to learn. Whiskey didn't think there was a single answer Justice could give him that would change anything. His gaze dropped to the gun he had taken off Justice. A goddamn gun.

"What do you do for Zander?" Whiskey surprised even himself with the calm note to his voice.

"I'm an accountant."

A loud sigh escaped Whiskey. He set the gun on the bedside table. Whiskey wouldn't ask again. Either Justice wanted to save them or he didn't.

"I really am his accountant." Whiskey turned his head and met Justice's stare at the claim. Justice didn't look away. "It's just not money I'm accounting for."

At Justice's words, Whiskey turned sideways, focused fully on Justice, and waited.

Justice visibly swallowed and looked away. He stared at the ceiling. "I don't know how much you know about Gio Conti, but he was a sick and twisted bastard. Most people know he brought Russian fighters here to start his underground fighting club that eventually turned legal MMA. What most people don't know is that he brought small children here as well." His gaze slid back Whiskey's way. "Some were pitted against each other in matches a lot like cock fights. The others were sold to the highest-bidding pervert."

Whiskey felt sick. He didn't know what he had expected from this, but it wasn't what he was hearing.

Justice didn't stop. "Most of those children are grown now, the ones who lived anyhow. Some aren't. Since the Conti's death, Zander has worked to find them. A few he's found good homes, others he's paid for counseling and college or just paid." Justice swallowed and looked away again. "Some he has given jobs."

"You do realize this should be my job, right? That's what I'm here for—the police. Not some gazillionaire who feels guilty."

A snort escaped Justice. It sounded bitter as hell. "Nobody has time to wait on red tape." His gaze latched on to Whiskey and didn't move. "Can you go to any state and pluck a child from a predator? If you could, then what? Will you slap them on the wrist while the child gets deported and put up for resale? You have no idea how deep this goes or how ugly it is. I wouldn't want you to know. Do you think Gio was the only one? The only reason you're hearing any of this is because I don't want to lie to you."

Something inside Whiskey snapped. He climbed on the bed, straddled Justice's hips, and stared down at Justice with all the rage in his heart. "But you did lie. For months. I don't know you at all. For fuck's sake." He dug inside his pocket and pulled out the ring box he hadn't stopped carrying around since he'd bought it. Whiskey flipped it open. "I got shot buying you this fucking ring, Justice." He swallowed past the helpless fury. "I wanted to marry you, goddamn it. All I was waiting for was the right moment to ask. Would you have said yes? Would you have married me with your fake name and phony job? How long did you plan to let me play the fool?"

Justice's gaze hadn't wavered from the ring since the moment Whiskey popped open the box. His chest rose and fell with rapid breaths, making Whiskey wonder if he was about to hyperventilate.

A growl escaped Whiskey. "Fucking answer me."

Justice's gaze snapped to his. He looked half crazed. "Yes."

Whiskey wanted to punch a hole in the wall. "Yes, what?"

"Yes, I would've married you," Justice answered without an ounce of shame tinting his voice. "I would've married you so goddamn fast, you wouldn't have known what hit you. If you would've given me a chance, I would've taken everything you offered with zero regrets because we are real. No matter what you tell yourself or how angry you are, you know damn well that we are the real deal. You know that I love you. You feel it or I don't for a second believe you would be here right now. *I love you.*"

The last wave of Whiskey's temper hit its highest pitch. His fist shot out, colliding with the headboard and cracking the wood. Every breath Whiskey took came harder than the last. Justice never looked away.

It was obvious he was ready to accept whatever fit of rage Whiskey threw his way, because it was true. They were real.

Whiskey collapsed. His body melted into Justice. With the ring box clutched in his hand, Whiskey settled onto Justice's chest. His heart beat steadily against Whiskey's ear. Whiskey had never felt weaker or more pathetic. Falling in love with Justice had done a real number on Whiskey. His eyes burned. He was tired. Whiskey didn't want to keep talking. There was no other choice.

"Why you?" Whiskey took a breath. "Why do you have to be the one?"

"Because life is cruel, angel. No one knows better than me that you deserve someone else."

A humorless laugh escaped Whiskey. "Actually, I meant, why do you have to be the one who searches for these children?"

Justice's chest expanded. Whiskey heard him take a deep breath. "Because I was brought here to fight as an adult, but my little brother was sold. He didn't survive. I did. I owe it to him to find the rest and make it right."

Whiskey crawled from the bed while doing his best not to meet Justice's stare. He shoved the ring in his pocket and pulled out his keys. While carefully avoiding looking at Justice, Whiskey unlocked the cuffs.

"Did you change your mind about arresting me?"

Whiskey toyed with his keys, incapable of focusing on Justice. "I don't have the authority to arrest anyone anymore. I quit my job this morning." He finally managed to meet Justice's stare. "For you."

Justice sat up. "I don't understand."

"Easton said he would dump his bakery in a heartbeat if Nico asked him to quit, and I realized I feel the same." Whiskey swallowed past the lump growing in his throat. "I don't want to save myself." The confession came out in a rasp. "But I'm so goddamn mad at you that I don't know how to get past it." To Whiskey's horror, his voice cracked on the words. Tears filled his eyes, but he refused to be that weak. He had already been the fool. He looked away and prayed for help. Justice had to save them, because Whiskey didn't know how.

WHISKEY'S PAIN WAS A KNIFE IN JUSTICE'S throat. He had done this. All Whiskey had done was love him, and Justice had destroyed him for it. The worst part was, Justice had no intention of stopping.

As long as Whiskey kept coming back for more, Justice would take everything.

"Come here." Even Justice heard the hard edge to his voice.

Whiskey's gaze snapped to his.

Justice pointed to the spot between his feet. "Here. Now."

Whiskey bit his bottom lip and shuffled closer. The instant he was within striking distance, Justice snagged his waist and hauled Whiskey between his knees. He held Whiskey's stare as he leaned in and kissed his stomach.

"Get my ring."

Whiskey dug the ring from his pocket again. His hands shook. Justice couldn't love him more.

"Ask."

For a moment, Whiskey stared at him in silence. Justice was scared as hell, but he refused to show it. He loved this man and Justice would do right by him always. Finally, Whiskey dropped to his knees. He stared at Justice with his heart in his eyes.

"Will you marry me?"

"It's okay if you need to be mad at me, but you'll do it as my husband." He leaned close, holding Whiskey's stare. "And I will be the greatest husband you could ever dream to have. I will never let you regret taking another chance on me. You mean everything to me. Tell me what you need from me to make this right and it's yours." Justice took the ring from the box and put it on, surprised to find it was a perfect fit. It was a sign. He cupped Whiskey's face, forcing his eyes away from the gold band. "Tell me you love me."

"I love you," Whiskey said obediently.

"I love you too, baby. You're perfect." He brushed his thumb across Whiskey's bottom lip. "Let me see your wounds. I've been worrying myself sick about your health."

Whiskey sat back on his heels and peeled his shirt off. Justice inspected both places where Whiskey had been shot, reassuring himself Whiskey had still been taking care of himself without Justice around to nag. Once he was satisfied, Justice pressed his lips to Whiskey's stomach and inhaled.

"Whiskey." Even Justice heard the pain and desperation in his voice. "I don't want to go back to being completely alone in the world again. I'm sorry I ruined everything."

The buttons loosened on Justice's shirt, making Justice realize Whiskey was quietly undressing him. "I just need to feel your heart beating against mine. Your skin against mine." Whiskey's quietly spoken confession was like a shot of adrenaline. A shot of hope. Justice let Whiskey have his shirt. Once he was bare from the waist up, Whiskey crawled onto the bed, forcing Justice onto his back before straddling Justice's hips, and covering Justice's body with his. Whiskey sighed as he settled on Justice's chest, as if he had been waiting for a thousand years to hold Justice. He buried his face in the crook of Justice's neck and held on. His every breath brushed Justice's skin. Justice closed his eyes. He hadn't slept since Whiskey left. All he did was pace the floor and follow Whiskey everywhere he went. Justice was exhausted. Holding Whiskey was his version of heaven. He loved the way Whiskey smelled. Justice swore that even Whiskey's body temperature was perfect for him. Whiskey was a big guy. Justice didn't feel the least bit squished. It was like they were meant to be exactly as they were—perfectly molded together.

"Whiskey?"

"Yeah?" Whiskey sounded every bit as exhausted as Justice felt.

"You're the only person who's ever loved me."

Whiskey's lips skimmed Justice's neck. "Sorry to be the bearer of bad news then. I'm also the last person who'll ever love you, because I don't share."

A smile tugged at Justice's lips. They would be okay. Maybe they still had a ways to go, but Whiskey hadn't given up on him. Justice could work with that. But first they needed sleep. Caring for Whiskey's health always came first. Everything else could wait.

A FAMILIAR SCENT TICKLED WHISKEY'S NOSE. His eyelids felt too heavy to lift. He was so warm and comfy. There was no bed in the world as perfect as the one he shared with Justice. Reality slowly crept back in. He had fallen asleep holding Justice. Whiskey had been scared as hell he would never have that again. But the truth was, as long as Justice would have him, Whiskey would keep coming back for more. Warm lips skimmed his jaw. A moan rose in his throat as love swelled inside his chest. His hand slid up Justice's back as he held Justice closer.

Whiskey hadn't let himself think too much. Truthfully, he had been too tired—mentally and physically—to think straight. Now, the full ramifications of everything that happened in the past few days sank in. He was unemployed now, and Justice... Jesus. Poor Justice. Had he ever seen anything but the ugliest parts of life? Whiskey had proposed. He had meant it too. Giving up his job was only the beginning. As long as Justice gave him honesty, Whiskey would give him everything.

"Tell me what I can do to help you."

A soft chuckle rumbled from Justice and vibrated against Whiskey's skin. "I'm doing the seducing here. I don't need help."

"And what a fine job you're doing, but that's not what I meant. Tell me how I can help you find these kids."

Justice froze.

Whiskey managed to pry his eyes open for Justice. Justice stared at him with his heart in his eyes. He looked hopeful—like he was scared to breathe wrong and lose Whiskey.

"Are you serious?"

Whiskey didn't hesitate. "Yes. I love you. This obviously means enough to you to risk everything, and I'm not the type to know something like this is going on and do nothing, so... how can I help?"

Justice unbuttoned Whiskey's jeans. "We'll find a way. Later," he said, sliding Whiskey's zipper down. "I love you so goddamn much." Justice's voice cracked on the confession. "I wish I would've trusted you. You deserved that much."

Whiskey held Justice's hand where he wanted

him and guided Justice into stroking his cock. "You'll make it up to me when you marry me. Until then..." Because no matter how much Justice thought he had coerced that proposal from Whiskey, Whiskey had fucking meant it. Justice would be his and make every untruth right. For now, Whiskey needed Justice to take away the lingering pressure in his chest.

Whiskey's eyes fell closed and his back arched as Justice skimmed his thumb across his crown. A whimper escaped him as Justice released him. He slowed down, peeling the remainder of Whiskey's clothes from his body. Justice looked calm. Serene. Whiskey couldn't tear his gaze from Justice's face. Maybe Justice would make him regret giving him a chance. Maybe he wouldn't. Either way, Whiskey had no other choice but to try. He loved this man. This one. For better or worse, no one else had ever stolen his heart. He wouldn't give up without a fight.

Justice didn't meet his gaze again until they were nude, and he had found the lube. Their eyes met. For a moment, they stared at each other in silence. Whiskey felt all the words that weren't said and that was the crux of the matter. Justice didn't often share his feelings, but Whiskey knew Justice felt him. Emotion poured from Justice's every glance and action. Whiskey knew Justice. He probably felt deeper than any man on the planet, but he didn't have words. Whiskey heard them anyway.

Lube squirted across his dick. Justice held his stare as he massaged Whiskey's cock, balls, and asshole, making him as slick as possible. Whiskey panted, incapable of looking away as Justice's fingers fucked his asshole just like Whiskey wanted his cock. Justice's intensity was hot as hell. He looked focused —like he could keep up this torture forever. Whiskey sucked air, fighting the urge to move. To fuck Justice's fingers. He wanted to fist his cock and take the orgasm he craved. Whiskey also never wanted this to end.

Justice shoved Whiskey's knees apart and crawled between his thighs. He stared down at his cock as he probed Whiskey's asshole, dipping inside and retreating. Whiskey clung to the sheets, trying not to explode. Justice massaged Whiskey's cock with one hand while guiding his dick inside with the other. He intentionally hit the hot button inside Whiskey that had him nearly doubling over in ecstasy with each thrust.

"You look like you don't know if you want to come or kill me."

"You're being a tease," Whiskey accused,

incapable of holding back the bitterness from his voice. He was ready to snap. His mind itched with need.

An evil-looking smile touched Justice's lips. "I believe in you. You can take it." At the claim, Justice slowed, dragging out each thrust. His hold on Whiskey's cock loosened until he barely rubbed Whiskey's dick.

Whiskey ground his back teeth to a pulp while he fought to take what he wanted. A growl rose in his throat. Just when he thought he would snap, Justice slammed inside, taking his ass hard. He squeezed and pumped as he stabbed Whiskey with his dick over and over, hitting at just the right angle. Whiskey took turns sucking air and holding his breath. Everything went silent—like the world held its breath. Whiskey's muscles tensed. Pleasure slammed into him, stealing his breath. A loud cry tore from his throat as wave after wave of ecstasy overcame him. Jets of cum flew through the air. Justice didn't stop beating at his cock, squeezing out every drop. He threw back his head. The muscles in Justice's neck stood out as he openly fought to reach the same level of pleasure as Whiskey. A gasp escaped him. His chin dropped. Justice's ice-blue stare locked on to Whiskey. His nostrils flared. He didn't look away as he pumped Whiskey's ass full of cum. In that moment, Justice had never looked sexier. Whiskey's chest swelled with pride. Soon, this man would be his husband, and Whiskey wasn't ashamed. He couldn't wait for the world to know Justice owned him. Whiskey had never felt freer.

EIGHT

IT SEEMED odd as hell to be meeting Zander Kapra under friendly circumstances. Not that Whiskey hadn't always found Zander amicable. Zander always cooperated and treated him with respect as a cop. Now he was meeting with the man as Justice's husband. It was weird.

Zander's huge guards stood watch as Justice and Whiskey cleared Zander's office door. The two who had always been stone-faced in the past smiled and nodded as they passed. Things got odder by the second. Before Whiskey had time to recover from one surprise, he spotted Leo huddled behind a laptop on the leather couch in the corner with a guy who couldn't have been more than twenty.

The pair looked up. Leo flashed his brightest

smile. "Hey, man. I'm ecstatic you've decided to help us."

Whiskey didn't know what to say. He shook his head, trying to shake off his shock. "Are you being serious? How long have you known about all this? How long have you been playing both sides?"

Not an ounce of shame crossed Leo's features. "It's all the same side, man, but three years. We've done a lot of good. Saved a lot of people."

The young one at Leo's side pushed his glasses up his nose and nodded Whiskey's way. "Hi. I'm Adrik."

He looked like a scared mouse. Whiskey nodded back. "Nice to meet you. I'm Whiskey."

"Congrats on the marriage. You both look really happy."

He was sweet. Adrik also looked shy and like he hoped to melt into the couch now that everyone was focused on him. "Thank you." Whiskey kept his voice soft, hoping to set Adrik at ease. Leo shifted slightly, somehow managing to get even closer to Adrik, as if protecting him. Whiskey had questions. He decided to hold them for Justice later.

Zander sailed inside the room with a huge guy on his heels followed closely by his guards.

"Oh, good. Everyone is here." He flashed

Whiskey a smile. "Thanks for coming. This is my husband, Maverick," he said, motioning toward the dark-haired man with honey eyes who had followed him in. He winked as he claimed the seat behind Zander's desk and hauled Zander into his lap as if he weighed nothing.

"It's good to finally meet you. Zander's been worrying himself sick that he had helped ruin your relationship by giving Justice a job. I'm glad you're willing to help us out."

"Are you part of the team too?"

Zander's eyes flashed dangerously at Whiskey's question, showing the first real hint of the man who ran the west coast. "No. It's Maverick's job to win as many titles as possible. Enough innocent people have been exposed to Gio's ugliness for one lifetime."

Whiskey supposed exposing him to it didn't count, considering he had already worked for years dealing with the dregs of society.

Zander got down to business, telling them about a man Pytor and Yaro had interviewed in Colorado. That man had given him names. Adrik and Leo manned the laptop, fussing like kids over what search words to add while researching the list of names online, cross-referencing social media accounts and whatnot. Whiskey watched everything everyone did with a detective's eye. Pytor and Yaro were a couple. He surmised as much within minutes. They cast each other heated looks when they thought no one else watched. Zander and Maverick talked in quiet tones, making plans to go to the Paralympics in Tokyo to watch someone they knew compete. Adrik wanted to be seen as equal to everyone in the room. Leo wanted to be seen by Adrik.

Justice touched his arm, pulling Whiskey from his observations. "They're just people," Justice said in a low tone meant for only Whiskey's ears. It was funny. Sometimes he thought Justice could read his mind. He'd been uncomfortable about this meeting, but Justice was right. Vigilante cause aside, they were all just people.

Whiskey's shoulders relaxed. "I know." As he made the claim, Whiskey realized how true the words were. He was fine with this. They would make this work. Going into the day, Justice had offered to quit if Whiskey didn't think this was a cause he could support. Now he realized exactly how fine they would be. In truth, it didn't matter what they did. They were in this life together no matter what. Their love eclipsed everything.

But he had said he would help. "We should talk to the contract killer who took out Gio," Whiskey said, deciding there was no time like the present to throw his skills into the mix. Everyone stopped to stare at him. Whiskey didn't back down. "Professional hitmen rarely take down a target without gathering every scrap of dirty laundry on them first. It's possible he has a full list of names—children and adults."

Zander stared at him stone-faced. "How did you know the Conti were wiped out by a contract killer? I wasn't aware anyone knew that. Officially, his death was ruled an accident."

Whiskey blinked, trying to look as innocent as possible. "I know. My brother is the one who closed the case in Vegas. He ruled their deaths as an accidental house fire. The world is better without Gio or his family in it. Sometimes, even a good cop has to look the other way."

A loud snort escaped Zander followed by an even louder laugh. His swiped at his eyes and shook his head before meeting Whiskey's gaze again. "Dmitry Salko lives a quiet life in the middle of nowhere about an hour outside Vegas. I can't imagine he'll appreciate a cop, even an ex-cop, showing up to question him."

Whiskey glanced around the room. Everyone stared at him, waiting. His gaze landed on Adrik.

"You should be the one to go." He was the best choice. The harmless choice.

Adrik didn't look away. "Okay."

"Like hell," Leo spat, taking Whiskey by surprise with his fury. "You're fucking insane if you think I'm letting you go to Vegas to interview a psychopathic hitman."

In an instant, Adrik transformed. He pushed his glasses up his nose and squared his shoulders. "Let me? I know you didn't just say you wouldn't let me. Who the fuck are you to allow me any damn thing? I'm a part of this team. And Whiskey is right. I'm the best choice for this."

Pytor chuckled. His Russian accent thickened with his laughter as he leaned Whiskey's way. "Starting shit on your first day, eh? You will do good things here."

Neither Leo nor Adrik paid anyone else any mind. They were too busy squaring off against each other.

"I'm your legal guardian and you live under my roof. You're not going."

Adrik snorted. "You *were* my legal guardian—for like six months before I turned eighteen. I'm twenty now, and I'm going."

"Well, you're not going alone," Leo said, refusing to back down.

"All right," Zander said, coming to his feet. "Adrik, you will head out tomorrow to question Dmitry. Leo will go with you but only to follow at a safe distance and keep watch. He will not approach Salko. Dmitry is not only dangerous because of what he does, he's also happily married, and will do anything to protect his family. Adrik is the only one of us who poses no threat."

"Part of me wants to be insulted," Adrik muttered, making Whiskey smile.

Zander motioned everyone toward the door. "I just wanted to touch base and get ideas for our next move. We have that. Please, go away now and find something fun to do with your day." He turned toward his guards. "That goes for you two as well. I have Maverick to watch my back."

Pytor and Yaro put up a halfhearted argument as they followed Whiskey and Justice from the room. Zander closed the door with a definite snap behind them before anyone could truly bitch. It was as simple as that. Whiskey should have believed harder in Justice and his innocence.

A huge grin spread across Yaro's face. "Maverick

will be watching his back all right. Never seen two handsier men in my life."

It was a claim that was negated by the way Yaro pinched Pytor's ass. Pytor chuckled as they walked away, reaching for each other's hands.

Justice pulled Whiskey to a stop. "Yaro only believes that because he hasn't seen us in action," he growled as he crowded Whiskey's space and captured his mouth.

Whiskey melted beneath Justice's touch. "Thank you," Justice whispered between kisses.

Whiskey leaned away but clung to Justice's chest. "For what?"

Justice shrugged, but he looked uncomfortable. "Trying, I guess. Meeting me ninety percent of the way because I don't have fifty to give."

A smile tugged at Whiskey's lips. Justice had such a dark view of himself. He didn't see what Whiskey saw. Justice loved him. For real. No holding back and that was worth more than anything else. "You know, I think I recall you threatening me with a blow job in your office once, but you never delivered."

Justice sucked a hiss through his teeth. "I can't have my super sexy husband thinking I don't deliver on my threats or promises. You might turn into quite the handful."

"Oh, I'll keep your hands full," Whiskey said, maneuvering Justice across the hall to his office. "But I definitely won't make it home. You're too damn delectable."

"God fucking damn, I love you," Justice muttered as he claimed Whiskey's mouth and hauled him inside his office. This was why Whiskey couldn't quit him. No matter what anyone believed about the man he had married the first minute he could, Whiskey knew the truth. This was love, and no one got to choose when, where, or who. But every day, Justice and Whiskey chose to fight for each other. Whiskey wasn't scared of Justice's darkness. It wasn't every man who would kill to keep him. It was shamefully empowering to be loved that hard. Whiskey would never give him up.

**Please keep an eye out for the next Sugar Daddies book, *Sugar Hero*. I know that I'm pretty quick to add a trigger warning to books, because—as a survivor—I'd never want to accidentally trigger anyone with my words. With that said, Adrik's story is next and his story will be harder to read than most. His past is horrible and ugly, but I have to stay true to him, so he can have the happy ending he deserves.

Thank you for sticking with this series. I love it and will keep writing it for as long as I keep loving it. I appreciate all of you.

Please consider leaving a review at the retailer where this book was purchased. Reviews really help with a book's visibility, which ensures I can continue writing. Thank you, Charity.

ABOUT THE AUTHOR

Charity Parkerson is an award winning and multi-published author with several companies. Born with no filter from her brain to her mouth, she decided to take this odd quirk and insert it in her characters.

*Eight-time Readers' Favorite Award Winner

　*2015 Passionate Plume Award Finalist

　*2013 Reviewers' Choice Award Winner

　*2012 ARRA Finalist for Favorite Paranormal Romance

　*Five-time winner of The Mistress of the Darkpath

Connect with her online:

--Join my street team: facebook.com/TeamCharityParkerson

　--Sign up for my newsletter: http:// bit.ly/CharityNews

　--Website: charityparkerson.com

--Facebook:
facebook.com/authorCharityParkerson
facebook.com/TheMenofSin
--Twitter: twitter.com/CharityParkerso

www.ingramcontent.com/pod-product-compliance
Lightning Source LLC
Chambersburg PA
CBHW060229180626
46813CB00007B/3015